The Imagination Box:
A Mind of its Own

Martyn Ford

FABER & FABER

First published in 2017
by Faber & Faber Limited
Bloomsbury House, 74–77 Great Russell Street
London, WC1B 3DA

Typeset in Garamond by M Rules
Printed and bound by CPI Group (UK) Ltd, Croydon, CR0 4YY

A CIP record for this book is available from the British Library

ISBN 978-0-571-33221-2

FSC
www.fsc.org
MIX
Paper from
responsible sources
FSC® C020471

2 4 6 8 10 9 7 5 3 1

ABOUT THE AUTHOR

Martyn Ford is a journalist from Hampshire. He likes cycling and enjoys pressing keys on his laptop until stories appear. This is the third novel in his trilogy for young readers (9+).

ALSO BY MARTYN FORD

The Imagination Box
The Imagination Box: Beyond Infinity

Reality leaves a lot to the imagination.

JOHN LENNON

Prologue

The man stepped inside the white tunnel, following its curve with his cautious eyes. Could he feel the electric thrum on his skin, he wondered, or was it just in his mind? The high-tech metal detector scanned him with a network of faint red light, then it beeped and a green bulb glowed above.

'Head on through,' the guard said, glancing up from his newspaper.

Everything was cleaner and newer than he had expected. Not that he had ever been inside a high-security prison before – but he'd seen films. A second guard ushered him through another checkpoint – this one was a little more like what he'd imagined: there were metal bars and a heavy lock which clacked and echoed and smelled cold.

'Cell 33 is at the end of the hall,' this guard said. 'Stay behind the yellow line at all times.'

The man made his way down the corridor, between two wide, painted stripes on the floor. He supposed they were for safety, to keep dangerous prisoners at arm's length. After a short walk he arrived.

There he was, the person he'd come to see. Fredric Wilde was lying on his bed, with earphones in, nodding along to music. The man tried a cough but got no response – a second and third attempt and still … nothing. So he checked up the hall, to make sure the guard wasn't looking, then leant forwards over the safety line and tapped, *clink-clink-clink*, on the metal bars.

Hearing he had company, Fredric turned his legs out and stood with a bounce. He approached the edge of his cell. They faced one another in silence, Fredric still nodding and swaying along to the song only he could hear. Once it was finished, he pulled his earphones out.

'Sorry man,' he said, in his rich American accent. 'I've rediscovered the classics. All this time on my hands, you see.' Fredric was wearing jogging bottoms and a loose T-shirt, both as grey as the thick concrete walls surrounding him.

'My name's Stephen.'

'I know who you are,' Fredric said. 'You like music?'

'Um, yeah ... I guess.'

'It's the only time I feel OK, at peace, when I've got my music on,' Fredric said. 'It's all I have left.' There was a pause. 'Well, that and the occasional bit of gossip. Is it true? That old teleporter of yours? Up and running again?'

Stephen Crowfield nodded.

'Oh, I bet your dear mother is *very* upset with you.' Fredric smiled. He then held his fists together, and opened them like a flower. 'Poof. Gone ... to make someone *disappear*. To ... delete them from the world, and then have them turn up again? What a thought.' His smile was now a smirk.

Stephen felt as though he was being mocked, and it made him angry – so angry his jaw ached from biting down. 'Look ... I need your help,' he said, calming himself.

'Not much I can do in here.' Fredric gestured behind at his cramped cell.

'You . . . you still have access codes, for the Nevada facility. We need them.'

'Um.' Fredric squinted, tilting his head. 'That place was destroyed, everything's gone.'

'Not everything.'

The two men stared at each other for a moment, through the bars. Hawk Peak Prison was near the sea – harsh, damp wind had chilled Stephen when he'd arrived, his cheeks were still rosy, his hair still matted. And it was so quiet now he could hear those furious waves out there, lurching up the rocks.

'What would you say if I told you I could get you out of here?' Stephen asked.

Fredric laughed through his nostrils. 'I'd call you a liar, and I'd tell you that Hawk Peak is the most secure place on God's green earth. Nothing gets out until the warden says so.'

'Believe what you want,' Stephen said. 'But decide, right now: are you going to help us, or not?'

Chapter 1

There was a sabre-toothed tiger in the playground.

Tim had just drawn what he reckoned was a perfect circle. Mr Hennessy, his maths teacher, had insisted they use a compass, but Tim found he could freehand the shape well enough. He was sitting towards the back of the class near the window, which breathed cold on his neck despite being shut.

As Tim wasn't quite as good at drawing straight lines, he slid his ruler from his pencil case to mark out the circle's radius. He held it up to his eyes, distorting the world in the diagonal, transparent plastic. Everything looked the same through the ruler, just in an ever-so-slightly different place. And it was at this exact moment Tim lost track of his conscious mind and strolled merrily into a daydream.

Wandering thoughts, he had come to realise, were extremely dangerous things. But it was too late. His heart thumped as he slowly turned to look out through the glass on his left. Then, with an itch of sweat and fear, he saw the large shape skulk from behind the bike stands – a low feline shadow emerging on to the tarmac, surveying its new world.

As discussed, there was a sabre-toothed tiger in the playground.

Its thick coat, heavy paws and tusk teeth – a pair of pale pickaxes, curved, deadly – were unmistakable. Yep, Tim thought, squinting, swallowing, yep indeed. That was certainly a sabre-toothed tiger. No doubt about it.

He realised he still had the plastic ruler to his eye, so lowered it and sighed, preparing himself for trouble.

Of course, just how this happened probably needs some explanation. To an outsider, Timothy Hart was just a regular twelve-year-old boy. Not particularly worthy of note, not interesting enough to remember should you see him walking down the street on some idle Tuesday afternoon. But, much like any stranger you might pass, things were very different up close.

It'd been over two years since Tim had first found the imagination box – a curious, botched-together cube of metal, about the size of a microwave but with tape and exposed circuits, flashing bulbs and the faintest smell of a warm, dusty computer fan. It was all prototype, all theory, all the ambitious work of an ambitious scientist. Back then, of course, it was called the thought-directed atomic construction device, or TDACD. It had seemed so simple and full of nothing but wonder. Even Tim, with his vivid imagination, couldn't have possibly guessed the problems it'd bring him.

There is a box. There is a box and anything you imagine will appear inside. That was basically the concept.

If Tim were to explain the gadget to someone – which he wasn't really allowed to do – they would probably go through a series of phases, just like he had.

Initially it is natural to wonder what you might create, what lovely material desires you might conjure.

Great, so you've got loads of stuff.

Now what?

Well, the usual progression for such a device – as is often the case with technology – is to expand on the idea, to stand on the shoulders of giants. In the case of the imagination box, that was exactly what happened. Thanks to an obscenely large amount of money invested by Fredric Wilde, of Wilde Tech Inc, a huge underground warehouse deep in the Nevada desert, previously used to construct airships, hosted the imagination space.

This was a vast open arena in which users could walk around and imagine things into existence right before their eyes. You could create a castle, a roller coaster, your own forest with original plant life and beauty beyond your conscious wishes. You could quite literally watch your imagination come to life.

But now, and this is where Tim's explanation would get a little more incredible, what if you didn't need the box, or the space, or any of the visible technology?

What if you could simply imagine something and it'd come into being? What if you could look at a table and think, 'I want a delicious piece of cake to appear there,' and a delicious piece of cake would appear there? Well, that'd be just brilliant. And – thanks to a series of frankly bizarre events, a dash of overconfidence and a smidge of misfortune – this was exactly the power Tim had. He was, in a sense, a walking, talking imagination box.

What, dear friends, is the worst that could happen?

For Tim, *one* of the worst things that could happen happened on a quiet Saturday morning back in May. With a lot of practice, he had managed to get his complete and total control over physical matter into quite an obedient order. He would create ketchup for his chips, he'd light candles as he passed, he'd add spiralling patterns to dull wallpaper, he'd even imagine increased air pressure beneath objects to make them levitate and, of course, he had pretty much everything he could ever want. But he found himself reminiscing.

He had been in the corridor of his home, the

Dawn Star Hotel, when he relived fond memories of the carpet that used to be there. The carpet that had a vibrant red pattern (which he'd pretend was lava) with interspersed swirls (which he'd pretend were stepping stones). It was a simpler time, hopscotching up and down that hallway. On the day in question, this nostalgia had softened his mind and relaxed his thoughts. He smiled at the memory.

A moment later, the hallway erupted – hellish roars of *real* fire, intense and loud and livid, had swirled up the walls and curled on the ceiling, stopping as though under his command right in front of his face. Tim had tried desperately to create water, or snow, or even sand, but in the panic he just couldn't concentrate long enough to make any of it appear.

Thankfully, although the damage was severe, the fire didn't spread. The hotel's owner and Tim's mu— . . . guardian, Elisa, managed to get the business insurance to cover the costs, blaming the fire on an unexplainable gas leak. What else, she said, could have possibly caused such a blaze?

'I'm so sorry,' Tim kept saying. 'I promise it was

an accident.' He was expecting some serious anger from her, but it never came. He offered to refurbish it himself, but Elisa said that'd attract too much attention – people had witnessed it after all.

'Stop apologising,' she said, wiping soot from his cheeks and checking his skin. 'No one was hurt, that's what matters.'

It had been almost five years since he came into the care of Chris and Elisa Green. Around the time they purchased the Dawn Star Hotel, they adopted him from his temporary home of Glassbridge Orphanage and started their family. Tim had been surprised that day, surprised they chose to adopt him, instead of a younger child. But, looking back, he was glad they did.

'Just think,' Elisa added. 'Just think how much I could get done if I had your mind.'

But, for Tim, this fire fiasco proved his new powers were unsettling. He was now dangerous – but dangerous by accident, which is often the worst kind of danger.

Now, here, in maths class, and again things had slipped. *This* particular lapse in concentration could be traced back to a recent school trip to the Natural History Museum in London. Tim and his best friend Dee had wandered the long, grand halls, gazing up and around, turning with open mouths. They'd filled in the worksheet and found all the necessary animals and exhibits – spotting everything from dinosaurs to the blue whale.

In the afternoon they had arrived at a large tank containing a lifelike sculpture of a sabre-toothed tiger – Smilodon to be precise. Both he and Dee had stared inside, through the transparent glass, at the extinct creature. It was this image – this moment – that Tim found himself remembering at the back of maths class on this fateful day.

There he was, plastic ruler still in hand, watching the creature stalk across the playground. The cat seemed calm, but then paused and lowered its stomach, perhaps picking up a scent, and headed towards the school building. Tim's breathing was fast, jittery. He turned to Dee by his side and squeezed her arm.

'Look,' he whispered.

'Hmm?' she said, her tongue protruding as she fiddled with her compass.

'Dee. *Dee*.'

She looked at him. 'What?'

Tim tilted his head towards the window. Dee's eyes widened – in an instant she realised what must have happened. She stared and mumbled what sounded like a swear word. When Tim turned back, the beast had ventured out of sight.

'Do something,' Dee said. 'Create something to stop it.'

'Like what?' Tim asked, feeling powerless now he couldn't see his creation. 'OK, let's—'

'What if it gets inside?' Dee said. 'This is a problem that can't be ignored, this—'

'*Is* this discussion something you would like to share with the rest of the class?' Mr Hennessy said. The teacher was tall and his voice deep.

'Nah, it's all right,' Dee said. 'You'll know soon enough.'

A loud scream echoed from up the hall. Heads lifted. Pupils exchanged confused looks.

'What was that, sir?' someone near the front asked.

Mr Hennessy stood and stepped across the classroom to investigate. A moment later a few students went barrelling past the now-open door.

'Run!' one of them said, tripping and scrambling away.

Then the fire alarm rang out above them.

'All right,' Mr Hennessy shouted over the noise. 'You know the drill. Single file. Calm. No running. *No running.*'

In the hallway, however, Tim and Dee found they were pushing through a panicked throng of teenagers and staff – blazers, ties and pale faces flashed past. And they were swimming against the current.

'Tim, Dee! You're going the wrong way,' Mr Hennessy shouted.

'We know.' Tim sighed. After all, this was his responsibility. He didn't really have a plan to stop the creature, but he knew he had to try. He was hoping he'd work something out by the time they arrived.

At the end of the maths block they heard a terrible noise – desperate screams and growls, bangs and crashes. They peered, then crept round the corner and saw the tiger. It had pinned an unfortunate individual, Jonny Harrington from Year 10, face down on the ground. It was mauling his bag which, much to Jonny's dismay, was still attached to his back.

'Call the police!' he screamed, getting thrust side to side along the floor as though the sabretooth was using him as a mop.

'Tim, do *something*,' Dee said.

'All right, quiet, let me think.'

He tried to imagine a cage, or a tranquilliser gun, or, or, or something. *Anything*. But, typically, his mind was blank.

Noticing this hesitation, Dee grabbed a textbook from the floor and threw it. The hardback spine hit the tiger's skull with a dull thud. It dropped poor Jonny and locked its green crystal eyes on them.

'It did *not* like that,' Tim said.

Jonny had crawled away and made it to his feet – he took off running past them.

The creature was flat on the ground now, edging forwards like cats do right before they kill something.

'Yeah, let's run away,' Dee said.

Tim looked behind as they sprinted down the empty corridor – the tiger was in pursuit, slipping and bashing into a locker unit as they took a sharp corner. At the next turning it pounced, its claws catching Tim's blazer, exposing the shoulder pad's foam lining. This sent him spinning, but he stayed upright and dragged Dee into a history classroom. He slammed the door shut and stepped backwards inside.

By now the fire alarm and tiger panic had completely emptied the school.

Tim and Dee armed themselves with a chair each as two double swipes of the animal's front paws turned the door to kindling. It flowed inside and paced the width of the classroom, never taking its gaze off them.

'Come on, Tim,' Dee said. 'Gotta resolve this ASAP.'

The sabretooth took three strides and leapt towards her. She somehow managed to roll under a desk, which splintered as the tiger slammed its long teeth through the wood, the points stopping an inch from her face.

'Oi,' Tim yelled, grabbing its thick hair and trying

to tug it away from her.

The heavy cat huffed and grumbled as it turned its body and clumsily pushed chairs to the side with its hind legs. Tim felt its fur slide over chunky bones. He released his grip and took a few paces back until he was near the wall, knowing exactly what would happen next.

With a throaty breath, the beast lowered its head and galloped towards him. It dived high into the air – its body huge at full length – and stretched out its front legs, every claw and tooth on display. The primal madness in its face seemed to stop time for a second. And, in *that* moment, Tim had full clarity of mind.

A logical solution.

In a blink the sabre-toothed tiger froze, literally encased in a block of ice in mid-air. The huge, bluish cube came crashing to the ground and slid at quite some speed across the classroom, coming to a stop and pinning Tim against the wall.

He sidestepped round and out, and wiped cold water from his cheek. 'Well, that was stressful.'

'Ice,' Dee said, lying amid a broken desk.

'Makes sense.'

The creature was stuck in that final striking pose and now seemed majestic, even beautiful. Even more so when the fire bell cut out and the classroom was silent.

'Hey,' Tim said, pushing the foam back inside his blazer's shoulder, 'it kind of looks like an exhibit in a museum.'

Chapter 2

The Dawn Star Hotel, with its black iron corner lights, grand old windows and golden frontage, looked well placed in the city of Glassbridge. Not many people can call a hotel a home but for Tim, the Dawn Star was the only place he'd ever felt truly comfortable.

'I feel it essential that I express mild, perhaps even moderate, disappointment,' Phil said. The tiny finger monkey was searching through a pot of pens on Tim's desk up in the bedroom they shared. He was lifting them out, one by one, and dropping them behind himself. 'I have been absent for great spectacles of both fire and now ice.'

The biros, although twice his height, were easy work. But some had rolled off the desk and Tim was dutifully clearing them up. 'You should be glad – either could have killed you,' he said.

'Why, of course, I am not implying for even a slice of a jiffy that subconscious arson is a positive thing,' Phil said. '*Au contraire*, by and large I think almost everything is better when not on fire.'

'Definitely,' Tim agreed.

'But the tiger? Oh, the tiger – hungry and incensed at its inexplicable existence, it must have been quite the sight.'

'What are you looking for?' Tim said, catching a rubber which the monkey had thrown over his shoulder with surprising power.

'My fine-line marker,' Phil said. 'It is in here somewhere. I just need ...' He grabbed a pair of scissors, climbed up and the entire pot tilted and fell – everything tumbling out.

'Be careful.'

Phil swept pencil shavings away and then scurried inside the cup. 'Not here. Not anywhere.'

Tim grabbed the pot and placed it upright. 'We'll buy you another,' he said, peering down.

'Heavens,' Phil gasped as he clambered to the rim, his furry little head poking out. 'Timothy, just simply make me one.'

'No.' Tim shook his head. 'No more. No more imagining stuff.'

'But I have work to do on the comic. You cannot – nay, *must* not – hinder my art.'

'It's too dangerous. I can't control my own thoughts.'

'Perhaps none of us can.' Phil's finger was on his chin. 'What a troubling notion … to be prisoners both *in* and *of* our own minds. Anyhow, usually I am a great admirer of such punctilious conduct but, with all due respect …'

The monkey carried on talking but Tim phased out. He didn't even know what 'punctilious' meant. Just last week Phil had celebrated his second birthday (or rather, more accurately, the second anniversary of the day Tim created him). It was a strange thought that something born from his mind had always known words he did not – stranger still to think that in human terms the monkey was only a toddler.

The comics Phil was referring to were

autobiographical – the monkey had documented the past two years, so all of his life. The first one, entitled *The Imagination Box*, was all about their first investigation. It told the story of Tim finding the imagination box in room nineteen, the guest suite opposite his bedroom. There were chapters dedicated to the moment Tim used the device to create Phil and the following challenge of finding the machine's inventor, Eisenstone, who had been kidnapped by Clarice Crowfield and the professor's former academic partner, Professor Whitelock.

The next was called *Beyond Infinity*. This one was about last year's events, which saw Tim, Dee and Phil (referred to in the comics as 'the team') discover that IcoRama mobile phones were being used in a network of mind control. The man behind the scheme, Fredric Wilde, was currently in prison, thanks to their efforts.

The latest edition didn't have a title yet (although Phil said he wanted to get the word 'mind' in there somewhere), but it was about everything that had happened since then, about all the things Tim had created with his new abilities. Phil had already pencilled in the Dawn Star hallway fire and had just that morning finished sketching the encounter with the sabretooth. For the monkey, all this madness was a joy – literally inspirational. His unstoppable enthusiasm wasn't dampened by the risk of death.

'... take Medusa, for example, her hair is made of snakes. How could ...' Phil was still rambling on.

But for Tim, things were different. Overall, his memories of the technology weren't entirely positive. This is not to say he hadn't had fun – he had enjoyed creating things at first. He loved playing in the imagination space, watching his castle appear, filling it with everything he'd ever wanted and much more. He had revelled in the praise he received for his abilities – impressing adults, especially ones he liked such as Professor Eisenstone, always felt good.

However, some other stuff did *not* feel good, like eventually getting bored of having *everything* – which he had compared to that tinge of disappointment you feel when Christmas is over. He'd learnt that looking forward to something is, quite often, better than the thing itself. It sucks, but it's true.

Also, he didn't like accidently creating monsters from his nightmares, nearly dying, nearly killing other people with jet-pack explosions, lava fires, large predatory cats and so on. He didn't like feeling scared of his own mind.

'And then there is the topic of unicorns,' Phil said. He was pacing now, up and down Tim's desk. 'Of course, they are armed with stings, but are they venomous?'

Tim had no idea how the monkey had arrived at this subject. 'Sorry, what?'

'Unicorns? Like horses, but—'

'Yeah, no, I know what they are,' Tim said. 'But you said they had stings?'

'Yes.'

'Well, no.'

'On their head,' Phil said, rolling his eyes.

'That's a horn. They're just magic horses with horns.'

'Forgive me, but I was under the impression unicorns were mythical, *id est* not real?'

'Yeah ...'

'Then, dearest Timothy, who are you to

declare the details of their anatomy with such steadfast conviction?'

Tim nodded with a pout. 'I'm glad you exist,' he said. 'You're my favourite creation.'

'That is a most gracious sentiment, and I shall accept your change of topic as concession in this debate.'

'Anyway, you don't have time to draw,' Tim said. 'We have to go.'

What Tim had said was true: he really wouldn't be creating anything else. In fact, Professor Eisenstone had scheduled a trip up to the Technology, Research and Defence (TRAD) agency in London to address the issue of his abilities. The fire was one thing, but the tiger had closed the school down, it had caused news coverage around the world. It was serious stuff.

The finger monkey climbed up the neck of the desk lamp and Tim held out his hand. Phil then ran up his arm and rolled across the front of his shoulder, landing smoothly in the top pocket of Tim's shirt.

Together they headed downstairs.

*

The headquarters of TRAD still impressed Tim, even though he had visited countless times for testing and brain scans. The skyscraper was huge and made from glass so clean it lived up to its name, the Diamond Building. Inside they worked on all kinds of amazing inventions, from teleportation to mind control, from imagination technology to cloning.

'Oh, Tim, Tim, Tim,' Professor Eisenstone said in the car when they pulled up. He ran his fingers through his grey, wispy hair. 'Thank you for agreeing to do this.'

It had been drizzly all morning. Now though, it was raining so heavily that the windscreen seemed to be flowing, as though they were in a car wash.

'No, thank you,' Tim said. He was relieved. Having to contain his imagination had begun to feel like torture, like holding his breath.

'But, but, it must be *your* choice,' the professor added. He removed his glasses and cleaned the lenses. 'Indeed, normal people have to work very hard to get things out of their imagination and into the real world.' He put his specs back on, blinked and turned to him. 'Are you sure you want to give this up?'

Tim nodded.

'Right, well, let's be fast,' Eisenstone said, lowering his head to gaze towards the rain clouds above.

However, Tim glanced once at the professor's lap and, with a faintly fizzy hiss, a black umbrella came into existence. Eisenstone laughed, looked down at the new item and shook his head in wonder. Tim would miss that face.

Bone dry, they made it inside the Diamond Building and TRAD's director, Harriet Goffe, escorted them down one of the many long corridors on the upper floors. They came to a door with frosted glass on the front. Tim read the name 'Rick Harris' along the bottom of the pane.

Harriet knocked once and they entered to see a cluttered workspace with all kinds of circuitry and gadgets scattered throughout. Rick also had a tall bookcase and, at eye height, Tim spotted the familiar sight of Professor Eisenstone's book, *The Future of Nanotechnology, Physics in a Quantum World*.

'Guys, this is Rick Harris,' Harriet said. 'Rick, this is Tim, and I think you've met Eisenstone.'

They did half waves and full smiles. Tim had heard his name mentioned in passing and knew he was one of TRAD's neuroscientists, despite being only in his twenties. But, most notably, he was the person who managed to fix Clarice Crowfield's broken teleporter – something Tim was keen to ask about. Rick had a long beard and an even longer moustache. It looked like the kind of facial hair that could be wound up to generate thoughts.

'And Phil?' Harriet asked.

The hairy head emerged from Tim's shirt pocket, turning left and right to take in the new room.

Utterly captivated, Rick's face transformed. 'Aye, your finger monkey,' he said, speaking in his low Scottish voice – his words seemed to bounce. He carefully held out his hand and Phil leapt down on to it. 'Oh, ha, wonderful.' He lifted him up in front of his face. 'It's fantastic, isn't it?'

'It?' Phil said, frowning, his tiny hands on his tiny hips.

And again Rick's face took on a new shape – his eyes opened as wide as they would go and he slowly pulled his head back, giving himself a double chin, his lips twitching in astonishment. He looked almost scared.

This always went the same way when new people met Phil. Even if you know what's coming, apparently *hearing* a finger monkey speak takes a moment to appreciate. However, after a short exchange, in which Phil complemented Rick on his 'most exuberant moustache', Harriet interrupted the excitement to discuss business.

'Rick has used the MRI scans of your brain to develop the chip,' she said. 'It's ... good work. I'll leave you to get it all installed.' Harriet said goodbye and left the room.

'That's right.' Rick handed Phil back. He then sat on his swivel chair and spun, dragging himself towards his desk with his heels. Beneath a suspended magnifying glass was a small silver device about the size of a micro SIM card. Rick turned back, holding it between his thumb and index finger.

'This wee gizmo will be gently implanted in your neck, just behind your ear.'

'In my neck?' Tim asked, feeling a little scared at the idea of something going under his skin. 'How exactly will it work?'

'Well, first you have to understand *how* your abilities are possible, how best to explain ...' Rick twisted the end of his moustache. 'Aye, so, now, remember in the imagination space, you would create a castle, or some trees, or anything a few metres away from yourself?'

'Yeah,' Tim said.

'You would look at where you wanted something, right, then you'd imagine it clearly and it'd appear? Now, the Wilde Tech reader worked slightly differently to Eisenstone's.' Rick gestured towards the professor. 'Eisenstone's *original* prototype used a conventional reader. It ... well, in layman's terms, it downloaded your thought, the image of what you imagined, and then, in turn, the box created it.'

The professor was nodding. 'Indeed.'

'Wilde Tech's reader was ... well, think of it as a projector,' Rick said. 'It read your mind and *projected*, as it were, what you wanted to create.'

'But the creations were real, solid things,' Tim said.

'Yes, perhaps *projection* isn't the right word – it's a tricky concept. I'm not even sure Fredric himself knew the details – he just paid some bright sparks to work it all out. Point is: the imagination space itself was simply a frame, a canvas, if you like, in which you could paint. But instead of paint, you were wielding all conceivable matter.'

'So, I could have used it outside, anywhere?'

'Oh, aye, definitely,' Rick said. 'If you had a functioning Wilde Tech reader you could *theoretically* make any room your imagination space.'

Tim's eyebrows went up. 'It's like an imagination box and reader all rolled into one?'

'Exactly that. I've looked at your scans,' Rick said, 'and I think our suspicions were correct. So, when you calibrated that Wilde Tech reader, you were stressed, correct?'

'Yeah,' Tim said. 'Very. I thought we were going to drown. We were trapped in the control room at Fredric's Nevada facility and water was flooding in. I felt . . . hopeless, powerless.'

'Well, then what happened makes complete sense. You inadvertently replicated the technology inside your own skull, or the biological equivalent, hence your abilities. It is extremely dangerous that this possibility was never explained to you. Of course, the technology doesn't know the difference between air and human flesh. You could have created anything inside yourself, or anyone else for that matter.'

'Whoa,' Tim said. 'So you're saying I created a Wilde Tech reader and built it into my own brain?'

Rick stepped over to a white glowing box on the wall and clipped in an X-ray of Tim's head. He could see the inside of his nose and the strange swirling pattern of his brain, like a cauliflower chopped down the middle. There were a few dark lines – which looked like veins, or tree roots – running amid the shaded grey image.

'Yes, and quite neatly too,' Rick said, pointing. 'It's woven beautifully throughout your skull – it's impressive that it caused you no harm. You said you felt powerless? So your subconscious created the necessary components to make you power*ful*. But, as discussed, perhaps *too* powerful. Of course, as you can see, *removing* the technology is impossible.'

'So, this new chip?' Tim said.

'Hmm.' Rick was stroking his beard now. 'The chip just transmits a very low-level signal that essentially disrupts the transmission in your head – basically turns off your abilities. So you'll be able to safely think about dragons and bird flu and plutonium without any risks.'

'Can it be reversed?' Tim had his first bit of doubt. Hearing Rick's explanation made him feel as though he might be making a mistake.

'I suppose, aye. If we discover a way to make the reader in your brain safe, we can simply remove the chip. I must say, I am sad to be the one to neutralise such a power – there is still so much to learn from this. If only I had your mind.'

Tim frowned – that was exactly what Elisa said to him after the fire. And then he had an incredible idea – a spark. 'You *can* have it,' Tim said, nodding, faster and faster.

Eisenstone was intrigued.

'Sorry?' Rick looked confused. 'What do you mean?'

'Well, you guys keep talking about not understanding how the human mind works, particularly mine. So, before you install the chip, I'll create a replica for you.'

'A replica?' Phil wondered – he was cross-legged on the desk, next to the chip. He was mimicking Rick's beard strokes.

'Yeah, a straight copy of my brain. Then you can study it to your heart's content. And … and then you could use it too,' Tim added. 'Of course, then you could make a relay with it or whatever and *anyone* could use the technology. That's always been the aim, right?' He turned to the professor.

'That *would* be a remarkable breakthrough,' Eisenstone said. 'But … but let's think for a moment, how would it work?'

Rick was nodding. 'It almost doesn't matter *how* it works,' he added, excited. 'Humans have been using technology we don't fully understand for millennia.'

'Indeed, but, but ethically …' Eisenstone was flustered – clearly uncomfortable about it.

'It's a genius idea, but do we have time?' Rick said. 'To create such a thing . . . How long would something like that ta—'

'It's done,' Tim said.

Rick turned. Sure enough, on his desk, just behind Phil, was a tall glass jar with a human brain inside. The wrinkled grey lump was floating in clear liquid and had wires coming down from where the spine should be, like a ponytail.

It was an ominous and unsettling moment. Rick looked like he had just found a winning lottery ticket. But Eisenstone's face was blank – the only reaction he showed was the slightest shake of his head. Silently, he disapproved. Seeing this, Tim wondered whether the object he was looking at was conscious. Could it think, could it feel? He remembered the clone of himself he'd created in the imagination space and how sorry he had felt for it, or rather *him*, when he was killed by Frederic. It wasn't difficult for Tim to imagine the fear and pain that doppelganger must have felt. He frowned at the thought. But this would be different, he told himself, catching Rick's eye. *This was just a brain.*

And Rick's bright smile chased those doubts away. Tim didn't say it out loud, but he knew the real reason he did this wasn't to help these scientists advance the technology. No, it was simply to impress them one last time.

Later that morning they 'installed' the chip in Tim's neck. Rick told them he had started his career as a medical doctor as he flicked a syringe and then sterilised a patch of skin just behind Tim's ear. It felt wet and cold, like minty toothpaste. Then Rick injected him with some local anaesthetic, numbing the area. He said it'd feel like a 'little scratch' which is an interesting lie doctors sometimes tell. In actual fact it felt like a piece of metal being shoved into Tim's soft, sensitive flesh. However, it was all over and done with in around fifteen minutes.

Rick showed Tim the tiny stitched hole in a mirror, as though he'd just had his hair cut. 'Very neat,' Tim said, turning.

'Now, test it. Try and create something.'

Tim looked at the desk and imagined a potato. He pictured its skin, the damp muddy smell, how it'd feel firm to touch. When he opened his eyes, there was no potato. He strained. He winced. Nothing.

'It worked,' Tim said. This was truly a bittersweet moment. He felt safe, but also as though he was now blindfolded, like he'd lost his favourite sense.

They cleaned everything up and thanked Rick. 'Harriet will be pleased,' he said. 'I've got some way to go to get into her good books after the whole Clarice Crowfield saga.'

'Ah, yes,' Eisenstone said. 'I heard about your work on the teleporter.'

Tim had been told all about Clarice Crowfield's return. He'd seen Stephen, her son, essentially destroy her in her own teleporter – a very vivid and well-drawn scene in Phil's first comic. She'd leapt into one of the chambers and Stephen – who had suffered years of abuse at her hands – pressed the switch. As the machine didn't work properly, Stephen knew she'd never reappear in the second chamber.

But then last year Rick repaired the teleporter's glitchy software. And the first thing to appear in chamber B was Clarice Crowfield, in the flesh.

'Harriet wasn't happy with what you did?' Tim asked.

'She was happy I fixed the teleporter. It got me a nice promotion,' Rick said. 'But she wasn't happy I let Clarice escape – especially as she managed to see a lot of TRAD's restricted areas first.'

'You just . . . let her leave?' Tim asked. 'Didn't you—'

'I *tried* to stop her,' Rick interrupted. 'And I tell ya, she called me some *pretty* rude names. I tried to calm her down, restrain her, but I didn't realise quite how dangerous she was. The second I lowered my guard, she picked up a stool and clobbered me round the head – knocked me clean out. But, hey, she can't stay on the run forever . . .'

Eisenstone was staring out of the window, through that howling rain, at the familiar London skyline. 'Indeed, I do sometimes wonder where she'll end up.'

Chapter 3

Tim sat down for dinner with Chris and Elisa up in their converted living quarters. This was a couple of guest rooms which had been connected and fitted with a kitchen, in a sense making a small flat on the eighth floor of the Dawn Star Hotel. Tim used to feel as though he was visiting someone else's house when he'd come up here, like an outsider, but nowadays he loved it almost as much as he loved his own bedroom. He loved the sunken brown sofa, the chipped coffee table, the smell that was simply of home – he loved all the ways it still looked like a hotel room and, more so, all the ways it didn't.

He helped clear the plates when they had finished. Chris ventured to the bedroom to pack his suitcase – he had a new job now, working with Elisa, at the family business. He would be heading away to look at and stay in another hotel. The Dawn Star was doing so well that they were considering expanding the brand. It was the start, Chris had said, of an incredible future for them all.

Tim was excited by this – he pictured a perfect new hotel, a large building in the countryside with a neat garden, short grass and places to hide. In his mind there was a rose arch and fairy lights wrapped around some of the trees – they would glow yellow and white at night. He was already looking forward to summer evenings at the new place, just drawing or hanging out with Dee and Phil near the flowers and in nearby woods. In his head, it would be like paradise.

At the kitchen sink, Elisa peered at the thin red scab on Tim's neck. She stroked a finger over it.

He shuddered.

'Sorry, did that hurt?'

'No, it tickles,' Tim said. 'I can feel the chip though, if I press on it.'

'How is it to be normal again?'

'You think I'm normal?'

'Ha, well, you're a little closer now.'

'Honestly, it feels great.' Tim had worried he might end up feverishly longing for things he couldn't afford now that he had to buy stuff, like a normal person. But he felt oddly free. 'I can still draw things, I can still make things. It'll just take a little longer. I dunno, maybe I'm growing up.'

Elisa nodded. 'You are wiser than your years, Tim,' she said. 'But you mustn't lose the fun.'

'Yeah, well, I've got a talking finger monkey. He needs regular attention.'

The previous night Phil had finished the final edition of his comic. The monkey still had pencil lead and bright ink – reds, blues, loads of green – spattered throughout his fur when he took to the desk to present his work. He'd propped the booklet up, beneath the lamp, and read it dramatically for Tim, Dee, Chris and Elisa – his shadow dancing across the panels as he acted out each part. When the monkey read the last page, in which Tim had the chip installed, he was standing quietly, looking to his feet with water in his eyes.

'And so we come to the end,' Phil had whispered. 'Adventures in our wake, we go on – like soldiers home from war, like the rich turned to poor, and wonder, once again, what it's all been for ...'

'Good, it rhymed,' Tim said. 'Probably a bit melodramatic though – why so sad?'

'I will just miss our wild exploits now that your imagination has been tied down,' the monkey had replied. 'Without them, I fear I will wander lost.'

Elisa washed the last plate and placed it in the drying rack. 'You do have to keep an eye on Phil,' she said. 'Make sure he's happy. You made him, you are responsible for his wellbeing.'

'I know.' Tim saw something in Elisa's eyes – something glossed over. 'You all right?' he asked, turning a bowl in a damp tea towel.

'Nothing, it's ...' Elisa leant on the edge of the sink. 'It's just ... you're lucky to have him. You created *life*. That's the most incredible thing anyone can do.'

'Yeah,' Tim said, nodding. 'I suppose.' He started drying a mug.

'I'll never know what that feels like.' A single tear

fell from Elisa's eye and trickled down her cheek. She wiped it away before it passed the level of her mouth then tilted her head back and breathed. 'Sorry.' Sighing, sniffing, she composed herself.

'No, it's fine.' This issue of being unable to have babies had come up a couple of times in the past. Elisa usually dodged the topic as it clearly made her uncomfortable. Once though, she had tried to explain how important it is for many adults and how painful it can be to learn you can never become a biological parent, so Tim wasn't shocked to see her cry.

But then she laughed, and Tim realised these were, strangely, *happy* tears.

'It's so weird how things work out,' she said. 'I used to cry myself to sleep when I'd think about infertility, or if I saw an advert on TV for baby food or something. That's why we adopted you so late, instead of a younger child. I just couldn't bear the idea of holding a baby that I hadn't carried myself. When the doctor first told me, it changed everything. I became a different person. I was … nervous, worried and stressed out with things that just don't matter.'

Tim had seen this for sure. There was a time you'd think the world was ending when Elisa learnt of a booking gone wrong or some pillowcases not being washed in time for the chambermaids.

'But it's a *good* thing,' she said, smiling now. 'I'm so grateful. I'm so relieved that I can't make children. It's truly a blessing in disguise, because it means ... it means I get to have you as my son.'

Tim was surprised but happy to hear her say that. He knew she loved him but, besides the odd hug and smile, she seemed to find it hard to express herself. And he could tell that sharing this meant a lot to her. He smiled back, but didn't really know what to say. His instinct was to make a joke, to make light of the situation, but he stopped himself.

A while ago, Tim had begun referring to Elisa as his mother when mentioning her in conversations. It was just simpler than saying, 'my guardian Elisa' or 'my adoptive mother'. People always asked so many questions. However, he'd never – *not once* – called her 'Mum' to her face. It had never bothered her, he didn't think, although recently he had got the impression she would probably appreciate it. He felt that this moment might just be the perfect time.

'Thanks …' he said, taking in a breath. '… Elisa.' He gave her a firm hug instead.

Maybe next time.

A few weeks later and Tim was back at TRAD. He had been called up to the Diamond Building for further readings and to check how the chip was working. Rick was in a good mood.

'Diagnostics seem fine,' he said, removing a small sticky pad from Tim's temple. 'Any issues? Accidently created any prehistoric beasts at school?'

'Nope,' Tim said.

'Aye, good, I'm pleased to hear it.'

They were sitting opposite one another in Rick's office. Tim spotted something over the scientist's shoulder.

'What's that?' Tim asked, pointing at a sketch of an awesome-looking gadget on the messy desk.

Coughing, Rick turned and moved a folder to cover it up. 'That's a wee bit of theory I'm working on … it's a, shall we say, *ambitious* project. It's, well …'

'Go on.' Tim was, and would always be, curious. What could a neuroscientist working at an organisation that specialises in incredible technology possibly consider 'ambitious'? Something worth knowing about, Tim thought.

'It's … it'll sound crazy.'

'Last summer my talking finger monkey created a horde of fire-breathing bear-sharks in Nevada.' Tim said. 'I'm pretty open-minded.'

'Fine, OK. Right, how to put it …' Rick grabbed a wooden board rubber from the desk and started cleaning his whiteboard. He wiped the final equations off with his sleeve, leaving just a few busy numbers and symbols smudged around the edge, creating a kind of blank cloud in the middle.

He drew a square, then pulled and twirled for a while on his moustache.

'That's a square,' Tim said. 'I know that one.'

'All right, so this represents the imagination box. When you created something–' Rick used a squeaky green whiteboard pen to shade in the square – 'you changed the state of matter inside. Do you understand? Don't think of it as *creating* an object, think rather that you've altered that piece of space and time. Instead of just air, you've made it so inside this place is a sausage, or a marble, or a—'

'Finger monkey,' Phil added from the desk.

'Aye.'

'Yeah, makes sense,' Tim said.

'This table.' Rick banged the wood. 'It's made of atoms, just as the air we breathe, just as your flesh and bones. As I said, you literally changed the form *you* take when you imagined that technology inside yourself. So it's the same with the *imagination space*.' Rick drew a larger square next to the first one and started to colour it in – this time he used an orange pen. 'You're changing the state of things inside.' He tapped the pen a few times on the board. 'But, as we discussed, it worked in a slightly different way.' Rick drew another square, this time red, much larger than the first two. 'How far was the range, before we installed the chip?'

'You mean how far away could I imagine things?'

'Aye.'

'Well, the tiger was the other side of the playground. I've made shapes in low clouds, maybe miles away?'

'From my calculations, I put it at a bit over a thousand metres, a kilometre – give or take,' Rick said. 'But what if there was no limit? What if you could look up at night and write your name on the surface of the moon, or make a star burn brighter?'

'What are you getting at?' Tim asked.

'Now.' Rick then used his sleeve to wipe away the edges of the red, third square. 'What if there weren't any restrictions on range or, and this is crucial, the *amount* of matter you could alter? What if you could change the material state of anything, anywhere, in an instant, just with your mind? What if it encompassed everything? Literally *every*thing.'

'Badger on toast,' Phil exclaimed. 'One could create a whole town . . . or even a whole new world.'

'Aye,' Rick said, nodding, staring at the wall. 'You could create a whole *universe*.'

'So, like, you could imagine a universe where the

sky is green and the grass is red?' Tim said. 'Or where everything is the same, but rats can fly and pigeons ... can't?'

'If ... if that was your preference.'

'Like the theory of infinity,' Tim said, thinking aloud, 'where every possible combination of physical matter exists?'

'That's it, aye. The implications on reality ...' Rick said. 'I think we're on the cusp of a new age.'

Tim stepped over to the drawing, looked back to Rick, who gave him a 'go on then' gesture, and then moved the folder aside to reveal it. Although the picture wasn't finished, the device was brilliantly sketched. It was a flat box, made of dark, brushed grey metal, with another taller box built on top. Rick hadn't added much detail to this upper section yet, but it looked like some of it was made from glass, or something see-through at least. Next to it was a heavy-duty reader – far bulkier than the imagination box's – connected by a thick wad of bound wires, which snaked a loop at the base. There was also a plug. Unlike Eisenstone's first prototype, this had no exposed circuit boards, no fiddly bits of technology poking out. No, it was neat and clean. However, all around the sketch, there were equations and scribbles, question marks and notes. Rick had been doing some big maths.

'Well,' Tim said, admiring the shading. 'It's a cool concept. What would you call it? The infinity machine? The universe maker? The world generator?'

'Hmm,' Rick shrugged. He stroked his palm over his mouth, slowly down to the tip of his beard. 'Or maybe ... the imagination station?'

'Nah,' Tim said, humming, 'call it ... actually ... yeah ... that is pretty good.'

'I, for one, submit that such a contraption should not be brought to fruition,' Phil said. 'I would draw your attention to the Greek myth of Pandora's box. Once opened, it cannot be closed.'

'Yeah,' Tim added, with a slightly nervous laugh. 'It could ... potentially mean wiping out our world, right? I mean, obviously you couldn't ... or, you know, *wouldn't* build something like that?'

'Pandora's box contained the world's evil.

Technology is neither good nor evil,' Rick said. 'It's how people use it that counts.'

'Sort of didn't answer the question there, Rick,' Tim said.

'Of course, no, obviously no. I wouldn't actually build the imagination station ... anyway.' He gave Tim a gentle tap on his bicep. 'Better get going lad. Harriet's gonna have me head on a plate if I don't get my work finished.'

Life and time sauntered on, months fell off the calendar. Tim's grades were good, his home life was happy, everything was going, for want of a better word, well. His friendship with Dee and Phil had actually *improved* now he couldn't create anything for them, which he could never have predicted.

But things, by their very nature, change.

An idle Tuesday evening came by and Tim was in his bedroom, tucked up nicely in his dressing gown and getting ready to go to sleep. He cleared away his drawing stuff, checked his phone and perched on the edge of his bed, brushing his teeth. One of the perks of having a bedroom that used to be a hotel room was that you were never more than a few paces from an en suite sink.

The TV was on, but the volume off, yet still the news caught his eye. With his toothbrush hanging from his mouth, moving slowly around his gums, Tim turned the sound up a few notches.

'. . . burning for a number of hours,' the news said. 'The cause of the blaze is unknown and countless firefighters from local and neighbouring services are tackling it both inside and out.'

The live footage cut to a skyline. One of the buildings, a tall one, was fully engulfed in thick, orange flames which glowed in each window and bellowed in fat swirls from the roof. A wide stripe of black smoke was disappearing into the sky, hiding the stars.

Tim's toothbrush was now completely still. He realised then that it was TRAD's headquarters, the Diamond Building, which was burning. What he didn't realise, however, was what this would mean for him come tomorrow morning.

Chapter 4

It's a strange feeling when you wake up somewhere you don't recognise. It sometimes happens after a sleepover, when you're far from home. Hotel guests often experience it for the first few moments of a new day.

Tim, however, was shocked to discover he *wasn't* in a hotel room when light warmed his eyes on Wednesday morning. No, he was somewhere else. Somewhere ... new.

The ceiling above was white and narrow, with a few flecks of bubbled, peeling paint. There were long lights too, one almost lined up perfectly with his bed. Only ... this wasn't *his* bed. It was too firm – hard springs and bobbly sheets. He sat up.

Wincing, he tried to remember what he did last night. Steadily, he began to feel quite sick. This became panic when, no matter how hard he strained his mind, he couldn't work out *how* he had ended up in this place.

'Right,' he whispered to himself. 'Calm down. Think. Where are you?'

He stood. This room was small, the walls were bare and pale blue. He had a wardrobe. He opened it and looked inside: clothes on hangers. Quite normal. He inspected them, sliding and clinking a few shirts along the rail. They were *his* clothes.

'What the … Phil, have—' He stopped himself, then stepped towards the bedside cabinet, relieved to have one. This was where Phil would typically sleep. He pulled the drawer open. Empty. 'What's happening?' he said, glaring in confusion.

The window.

Outside he saw a courtyard. Trees. A few benches. It *was* familiar.

'Oi,' a voice yelled from behind his door. 'Oi, Tim, you up?'

He turned and cautiously approached. Gritting his teeth, he gently opened the door, peering round. A girl he'd never seen before was standing there. 'Tim, I got this awesome— Whoa, you all right? You look pale. You look *awful*, if I'm honest.'

This girl was tall, taller than Tim. She had short spiky hair and was wearing an overly colourful patchwork jumper.

'Who are you?' Tim asked.

The girl smiled. 'I'm King of the Goblins. Who are you?'

'No. Don't joke. Really, who are you?'

'Stop mucking around, Tim. Come on, breakfast is ready, but I wanna show—'

He slammed the door shut.

'God,' she yelled from behind the wood. 'Rude.'

Swooping back to his bed, Tim started to search for clues. Pillow seemed normal. The mattress was a bit lumpy, but otherwise fairly reasonable. He looked underneath. There was a large wooden trunk, which he slid out and opened. It was full of *stuff*. Clutter. Magic 8 Ball, broken watch strap, playing cards, rubber chicken. He dropped things back inside. Loads of it was his, but some of it wasn't. It looked like someone had come into his room and taken items at random, then mixed them with a load of other nonsense.

He sat for a moment there on the floor, with his eyes shut and his hand on the edge of the wooden chest. Calm down, he thought, what would Dee do?

She would be logical. She would assess the problem and solve it.

Facts. What were the facts?

He was at home but then woke up somewhere else. How did he get here? Did he sleepwalk? Unlikely. Had someone kidnapped him? Maybe, but who and why? Was he dreaming? Again, could be the case, but it all seemed too vivid. Pinching is the classic test, but Tim gave himself a firm slap on the face instead.

'Ouch.' It just hurt – he rubbed his cheek. So he wasn't asleep.

Had he come here of his own free will and then forgotten? Possible. But how? Something would have had to screw with his memory, something like—

The chip!

Tim's fingers scrambled to his neck. He felt the scar and moved the small piece of metal around under his skin. It must have a glitch or something and it had wiped his memory. That's it. This thought, although dodgy, did settle his nerves. Very simple solution – he'd contact Rick Harris and get it sorted out. Can't very well be waking up in strange places.

Still, he wondered *where* he was.

The very second he stepped out of the bedroom door, a bright light above stung his eyes. It was accompanied by a weird, haunting wailing noise. The walls seemed to sway. The sound was coming from the multicoloured jumper girl who had knocked earlier. She was standing at the end of the long hallway holding a megaphone. She was singing into it. 'Tim, Tim, Tim,' she yelled. It seemed somehow too loud and echoed in his skull. 'Tim, Tim, *Tiiiim*.'

'Please be quiet,' he said to the stranger.

She lowered the megaphone. 'Sorry, I found this in the basement. I thought you might want to come down the pond, shout at some ducks?'

'Look, I don't know who you are, but can you at least tell me *where* we are?'

'It's not funny any more,' she said. 'You're actually being kind of freaky.'

He sighed. 'Just tell me.'

'We're in Glassbridge? Which is a town in England? Planet Earth?'

'Yeah, *where* in Glassbridge?'

'Do you want coordinates?'

He glared at her.

'Glassbridge Orphanage,' she said. 'Where you live?'

All he could think was 'no'. Just no. It felt as though they were on a boat and it had just been hit and lifted by the tallest wave imaginable – the walls lurching towards him, the ground falling away from his feet. He steadied himself and took a breath. But then he shook his head and told himself it was impossible. This girl was simply insane, he thought, and he had a sudden urge to get away from her.

'That's enough from you,' Tim said, turning on his heel and running off down the hallway. 'Crazy, crazy people,' he mumbled under his breath.

When he got to the bottom of the stairs, he realised that the strange girl was at least half right – he had woken up at Glassbridge Orphanage. He recognised it now. However, he had no interest in hanging about, so he decided to run home – he could figure things out there.

As he passed through Glassbridge, he felt dizzy again – he had a sort of lingering déjà vu. Everything looked the same, but different. The cars were all a bit strange, like they were from the past – they had a weird 1950s retro vibe about them. Big bonnets, bulbous curves, round headlights. However, they were shiny and futuristic at the same time. And, weirdly, almost silent – gliding along the road smoothly, as though on invisible rails. They were obviously electric, Tim thought.

On the high street, a double-decker bus stopped to pick up some passengers. The side of it was alive with a moving advert: a woman's eyes blinking at Tim, trying to sell him make-up.

People's clothes too – it wasn't that they were wildly different, but just as though fashions had changed overnight. Men's shirt collars were a smidge bigger, women seemed to be wearing more hats and everywhere he looked he saw little high-tech gadgets. Nearby, a man entered a block of flats, a camera scanning his eyeball for security. A tall policeman strolled past wearing sunglasses that had flowing text on the lenses – a digital head-up display, giving him information about the world.

And yet it was all familiar, all totally normal, at the same time. It was as though all of Tim's memories were wrong. The feeling was impossible to comprehend, impossible to put into words.

After the mile or so run, which soon became a jog and then a fast walk, he arrived at the Dawn Star Hotel, where he caught his breath and felt incredible relief, despite the sick, swaying feeling in his stomach. *Home*, he thought, as he pushed his way through the revolving doors. Luckily, this place just felt familiar. There were all the nice, comforting sights and sounds of the lobby – people checking in, a faint radio playing gentle music nearby, someone reading a paper on the sofa by the window. He went through the oak doors, along the hallway and ran upstairs, to the second floor, to his bedroom.

Tim had a bad habit of leaving his door unlocked, so when he pushed the handle and it didn't open, he banged his head and shoulder into it. Startled, he grabbed it again and gave it a real shove. It was locked. And then he heard that someone was inside.

He knocked, hard. Then again.

A man wearing a white hotel bathrobe, complete with the fancy little gold DS sewn on to the breast, opened the door. 'Yes?' he said.

'Who are you?' Tim demanded. 'What are you doing?'

'I was …' The man seemed confused. He pointed over his shoulder. 'I was having a shower?'

'In *my* room?' Tim said, pushing past him.

'Now hang on a second,' the man said, his tone different now. No confusion, just anger. 'You can't go barging into people's rooms. If there's been a booking mix-up we can— Hey!'

Tim tugged open the top drawer, expecting to find Phil in his miniature bed, but it was empty.

'But . . .' Tim whispered to himself, leaning closer and touching the bare wood on the inside of the drawer in case something was wrong with his eyes. He stood up straight, covering his mouth.

And then he noticed his bedroom had been redecorated. It looked bare, plain, just like any other hotel room.

'Aw, what is going on?' he said, turning full circle, grabbing his hair. The room kept spinning even when he stopped.

He turned back to the man, but he'd left. So Tim checked the closet, every drawer, even the man's suitcase, searching for any clues. By the time he'd finished, the room looked trashed.

'What on *earth* are you doing?' a voice said. It was Elisa.

'Oh thank God.' Tim ran and grabbed her, squeezing her hand. 'Listen, Elisa, something weird is going on. My room . . . it's . . .'

'This isn't your room,' she said. Elisa pushed him away, holding him by his shoulders.

'Yeah, I can see that. I've gone all wonky . . .

confused. I think the chip . . . it's messed my memories up or something.' Although still terrified, just having her nearby helped Tim keep his composure. 'Sorry about the mess,' he added.

'That's fine.' Elisa was glaring, though she looked worried. 'Where did you come from?'

'I . . . I was . . . I was at Glassbridge Orphanage.'

'All right. I'll call them, OK. Someone will come and pick you up.'

'What? No,' Tim said. 'I don't want to go back.'

'Listen, young man, I don't know what's going on, but—'

'Young man? Elisa, it's me, Tim?'

Hesitating, she turned her head slightly. 'I'm sorry, but . . . I think you've made a mistake,' she said. 'I don't know who you are.'

Tim was fending off tears now.

'But, you're my . . . you're my mum?' he said to her, for the first time in his life, his voice straining at the end. Although he'd said the words aloud, they somehow didn't seem to be true.

He knew her well enough – Tim could see that

Elisa wasn't joking. She wasn't lying. She really didn't recognise him.

'Listen, kid,' the man in the dressing gown said. 'You're in the wrong place, now help me clean all this up.'

'I . . .' Tim started, then he frowned. 'I have to go . . .'

'Yes, I think that's the best idea,' Elisa said. 'Have you a number for the—'

But Tim had bolted off down the hall, down the stairs, through the lobby and back outside. Panicked, he ran along the pavement, huffing as he went.

At the end of the street he bumped into an old woman who was riding a mobility scooter. Catching his balance, Tim held her shoulder and apologised. As she grumbled something and weaved off up the pavement, he saw that over her legs was a tartan blanket.

Tartan like Scotland.

Scotland like Rick Harris.

Tim shot down into an alleyway and squatted by a bin. Even the bins looked somehow different, he noticed, as he leant against it. He needed to get his thoughts in line. All the panic had clouded his mind. Right, he had to get on a train and go to London. That was all that mattered. Go and see Rick and get this chip removed or get a software update or whatever. Then it'd all be fine, he thought. Everything would go back to normal. It was all in his head. It was all in his head. *It was all in his head.* Tim rested the back of that mischievous head on the large bin behind him. It made a hollow donk sound. He turned and looked – the bin was square and made of dark grey metal. It reminded him of something . . . A drawing he'd seen.

He was breathing like he'd just emerged from deep water as he dared to think it.

A drawing of an all-powerful machine. A machine that shouldn't exist. A machine that—

'Oh no,' he whispered, resting his face in his hands.

He *knew* he shouldn't have trusted someone with such indulgent facial hair. Rick was too ambitious. Of course he built it. Of course, he wanted to impress Harriet, rise up the ranks at TRAD. The imagination station could change *everything*, create a world, a universe.

But how, Tim wondered, would a machine like that even be possible. Rick would need some kind of, some kind of—

Oh, *of course*. Rick had the replica of Tim's brain. He had Tim's abilities from the moment he made that copy. That's probably what that glass compartment on the sketch was for ...

This theory made at least a *bit* of sense. That'd explain the weird cars and clothes. Rick must have reinvented them, pictured everything this way. All for his very own universe.

After he'd calmed himself down, Tim peered back towards the street and began to notice all the other tiny differences, feeling a twitch of fear with each one he saw. It was a bit like being in another country. The font on the road signs was different, but he couldn't say quite how, the traffic lights were different, but again he couldn't say in what way.

Some of the buildings had a sort of eerie Gothic feel to them, built from big grey stones, covered in rough lichens and strange rashes of moss. Like a graveyard. And yet, at the same time, it was all modern, with neon lights glowing on shop fronts and high-tech gadgetry wired into everything, as though the past and future had fused together and turned Glassbridge into a truly foreign place.

Tim looked down at his feet. Even the tarmac was a slightly different shade, especially in the sunlight, which, like everything else, was odd – maybe a tiny bit bluer than normal? He put his hand out into a patch of light and opened his fingers, feeling the warmth. But it was subtle, he thought, like the blurry moment in a dream when you realise that something's *not quite right*, and yet continue to sleep.

Something buzzed near Tim, beyond a fire-escape ladder above, interrupting his thoughts. It was a weird drone thing – a little larger than a football, with spiked antennae, a flashing light and what looked like a camera. The hovering bot came down into the alleyway, then flew off and round the brick corner.

When it was gone, he checked his phone, which looked completely different to how he remembered – it was after 12 p.m. now. All this insanity had taken it out of him. He wasn't hungry, but he *was* thirsty.

Stepping back out on to the busy street, Tim could only wonder what kind of lavish life Rick had made for himself in this new reality. He was probably sipping cocktails on a beach somewhere, swinging in a hammock, watching the sun set over a still, crystal-clear sea.

Tim had to grab his forehead when he thought about it too hard. To think – everything, the pavement, the cloudy sky, the quiet cars that whispered past, even the earth itself. That bird. This corner shop Tim had arrived at. All of it had changed. *All of it* was new – all created in an instant by a machine Tim didn't understand. And yet, weirdly, so much was the same.

They still had water, which was lucky. Tim grabbed a bottle from the fridge at the back of the store, and queued to pay.

'That's one pound ninety-nine,' the clerk said, beeping it through the till.

Corner shop prices were still stupid, Tim thought. That's something.

Did he have any cash? He patted himself then

pulled out his wallet and felt it had no coins. However he *did* have a ten-pound note.

'There you go,' he said.

But, as Tim handed over the cash, he flinched – this was like a real sleep twitch, the sudden jolt that would have woken him up had this been a nightmare. He stood there, frozen, holding the paper, the clerk holding the other end, neither letting go.

A familiar face was staring up from his fingers – a portrait he'd seen before, a smile he'd never forget. The straight black hair, the skeletal cheekbones – that proud, proud gaze. Right there, right on the front of the crisp bank note, it was her.

Clarice Crowfield was on the money.

Chapter 5

Tim downed his water then threw the empty bottle in the bin outside. With a cold ache in his throat, he crossed the street. He was standing in front of Glassbridge cathedral now – the tall spires and stone arches towered above. The afternoon sun was low, shining both in and back out of the building, every colour of stained glass on the pavement at his feet.

'Excuse me,' Tim said as he grabbed the arm of a passer-by.

The man stopped and pulled his wireless earphones out. 'Hmm?'

'Sorry, I'm not from here and I noticed Clarice Crowfield is on the ten-pound note?'

'Yeah, she's on 'em all, mate.'

'I see,' Tim said. 'Why is that?'

'Cos she's the Prime Minister of the Great British Empire . . .' The nearby cathedral door opened and the jarring chords of a busy organ and a hundred voices from a choir echoed on to the street. 'Enjoy your stay,' the man said, as he left.

'What?' Tim replied, staring wide-eyed. 'Oh yeah, I'll try.'

After a few seconds, he stepped out from the glowing orange and green and blue light and did the dream test again, slapping himself in the face. Once. Twice. But nothing. This was real.

Not for the first time that day, Tim took off running. Except now he wasn't panicking. Well, he was. All right, he admitted, he was on the verge of a full-blown breakdown – part of him wanted to lie on his side, on the pavement, hug his knees and just rock backwards and forwards, screaming, until someone came and took him away. But, as well as this temptation, he was also finally getting some clarity. Today had been a bad day – maybe one of the worst – and the feeling he had, the dread terror of being totally and absolutely alone, made it ten times harder. It felt like he was in a suddenly wingless plane. Trapped, just falling and falling.

There were loads of problems that would need addressing, but the first one he had to solve was this awful loneliness. He needed a friend. He needed Dee.

Of course, however, he suspected she might not know who he was. That fear went back and forth in his mind until he arrived at Glassbridge Academy. It was a normal school day so everyone was in uniform, besides Tim. He worried someone would spot him and ask why he hadn't been in class, but then he realised he had far bigger issues on his plate. Plus, did he even go to school here? It didn't matter.

It was lunch break when Tim arrived – the playground was full of students, some talking, or playing football, or running about the place, yelling and laughing. Hidden in a nearby bush, he watched through a chain-link fence, scanning faces, spotting blonde girls through the busy crowd, searching and searching and—

There. There she was. Sitting alone on the back

wall near the field. Tim positioned her in his vision so she was perfectly framed in a square of fence wire. She was watching other kids playing and seemed sad, sitting all by herself. She looked kind of lonely – which was weird. Maybe she *did* remember him, he thought, hopeful. Maybe she was just worried about where he was?

He decided it was best not to get spotted by too many people so, after break finished, he walked quickly straight across the empty playground and in through the tall swing doors. Then he waited in the hallway outside Dee's tutor room.

'Dee, it's me,' Tim said, blocking her path as she came out.

'OK.'

'Do ... do you know who I am?'

'No.' Dee shook her head. 'Do you know who *I* am?'

'Yes. We need to talk.'

'We are talking.'

'Somewhere private.'

'Why?'

Tim looked over his shoulder. Right behind him was a stationery cupboard. He pulled the door open and guided Dee inside. She entered without protest, but was frowning the whole way.

'Not sure I'm all right with whatever is about to happen,' she said, as Tim clunked the door closed. 'Bad vibes.'

'Look, shut up a second,' Tim said. 'This is complicated. I am going to explain something now and it *will* sound insane. Here we go: we are best friends, in … in another … it's a … well, it's a parallel universe.'

'Hmm … yeah, that does sound insane. Is this how you normally make friends?'

'No, seriously. Right, just listen a sec. I know you. I know you well. Your name is Dee Eisenstone, all your clothes have polka dots, your mother is called Sarah, your grandfather is a scientist, a theoretical particle physicist – he's called George. He has a watch with the letters PE carved on the back. It's silver. You've lived in Glassbridge your whole life. You're completely rational, almost like a robot. You never really worry about anything. You always tell me that all problems can either be ignored or solved. You haven't got a favourite colour – you say they all have pros and cons. You sometimes kinda dance when you speak, like bob side to side a bit. You have a mole on your neck, behind your hair. You say you'd like to be a bit taller, but you admit you're average height for your age. You have a scar on your left knee from falling down some stone stairs when you were small, but you can hardly remember it. I could go on ...'

'You're a stalker,' Dee said, holding up her hands. 'Which is fine. I've never noticed you before and you seem mostly harmless, so who am I to tell you to stop? But I would ideally like to leave this cupboard immediately.'

'No.'

'No?'

'Please, let me explain.'

'You're keeping me prisoner in the stationery cupboard?'

'Of course not.' Tim faked a laugh.

'So I *can* leave?'

'I'd rather you didn't.'

'Noted, but will you stop me if I try?'

Tim nodded.

'Then you should have answered yes to the prisoner question,' Dee said. 'It's OK. I just want to know where we stand. Get the dynamic on the table, yeah? Hostage situation, got it.'

'Right.' Tim took a big breath. 'Your granddad invented something called an imagination box and ...' He then explained everything that had happened over the last two years or so, right up to this moment. Dee, to her credit, quietly listened to the whole story. '... and then I ran straight here, grabbed you and pulled you into this cupboard.'

'Is that ... are you done?'

'That's the lot,' Tim said.

'OK, well, loads of that was crazy, the monkey thing is just ... yeah ... But one bit stuck out: Clarice Crowfield, the actual *Prime Minister*, kidnapped my granddad a couple of years ago?'

'Yes,' Tim said. Then he winced. 'Well, no. I don't really fully understand how it works yet, but basically, yes she did, but not in *this* universe. She *isn't* the Prime Minister. Not really. I mean, she is now. But not properly. In the *real* world she isn't. Does that make sense?'

Dee shook her head.

'So … like … for *you* it never happened,' Tim said, still piecing it together himself. 'But for me it did. I guess … I guess you're literally a new person. So you have a new body, a new mind, new memories too. Everyone does … God, that's mad to think, isn't it? That everyone has new *memories* as well. The physical structure of your brain has been changed. It's the only way it'd work. Isn't that *mental*?'

'Most certainly. Doubly so because *you* still have *your* memories.' Dee rolled her eyes.

'That's a sound point actually. Why not just create a universe where I can't remember anything?' Tim wondered. 'Unless she's punishing me for all that Crowfield House business? She *wants* me to see what's happened, to see that she's won. Oh, she is good. You've got to kind of respect that level of—'

'Lovely, great,' Dee said. 'And yes, I believe you, we can be friends.'

'Really?'

'Yeah, sure.' Dee stepped past him. 'I just have to get to class, so maybe call me later and we'll go for a milkshake and— HELP!' Dee yelled as she pulled open the door. 'SOMEONE HELP ME!'

Tim slammed it shut. 'Relax, all right! I'm telling the truth.'

'Look, buddy, listen to yourself. Would *you* believe such a story?'

Tim thought for a moment. 'Probably not,' he admitted. 'Not without some evidence.'

'That's the thing with outlandish claims, I'm afraid. Gotta be able to back 'em up.'

'I can.'

'Go on then, one ticket to proof town please. I'm a-waiting,' Dee said, bobbing her head. 'And a-one, and a-two, and a-three.' She put one foot forwards and lifted an arm for Tim to begin. He was frowning. 'Any time now, for the old proof. Proof-a-licious. Proofy McProoferson. Sir Proofalot, slayer of nonsen—'

'It's hard, because everything is different. But, then again, lots of things *are* the same. You're still here.'

'That I am,' Dee said.

'And your granddad is still a professor, right?'

'That he is.'

'Maybe he's … maybe he still has the prototype.' Tim was talking to himself now, and pacing as he did so. 'He dismantled it in the *original* universe because he was moving abroad, because the Crowfields were after him. That's why he was hiding out at the Dawn Star. But, here, none of that happened. He's never met me. As far as he knows, the machine doesn't work. And … and it'd use the old-style reader. I could still operate the box, even with the chip … I could … Yeah, *that* would prove it.'

'I … no way.' Dee was shaking her head, faster and faster.

'Yes.' Tim stood perfectly still now. 'We need to go and see your granddad.'

Chapter 6

'I am so, so sorry,' Dee said as they stepped through Eisenstone's front door, wiping their feet on the mat. 'Honestly, this is not a good thing.'

The professor was wearing his scruffy lab coat – which had rips and a couple of frayed, burnt patches on the sleeves – and he had a pair of safety goggles perched on the top of his head. He checked his watch. 'Indeed, you, you surely have almost an hour left of school?'

'That wasn't even what I was apologising for ...' Dee said, then she sighed. 'Granddad, this is Tim, Tim this is ... well, you seem to know who he is ...'

Like Elisa and Dee, Tim knew Eisenstone well enough – the professor really didn't recognise the young boy looking up at him. 'We have met, but you can't remember, because it happened in an alternate universe.'

'Ha.' Eisenstone smiled. 'I can certainly, certainly see why you and Dee are friends. Eccentric little child, aren't you?'

Inside, Eisenstone stepped into the kitchen, whereas Dee and Tim waited in the living room. They sat silently – Tim on the sofa, Dee on the chair. The professor's fluffy ginger cat walked in and purred as it rubbed itself against Tim's leg.

'This cat is called Jingles,' he said.

'We've covered this,' Dee whispered. 'Being a stalker isn't proof.'

'You kids want a drink or, or, or any food?' Eisenstone called from the kitchen. 'I have biscuits.'

'No, we're fine,' Dee yelled back.

'Good,' the professor said, returning to the living room. 'Because I don't have biscuits. You look like there's something on your mind.'

Dee lifted an arm to Tim, inviting him to speak.

'Right, Professor Eisenstone.' Tim turned

on the sofa to face him. 'You are a theoretical particle physicist.'

The professor smiled at Dee. 'Yes, yes, yes. My reputation precedes me.'

'You are an expert in the fields of nanotechnology and quantum mechanics,' Tim went on. 'Years of research has led you to build, I really hope, a machine called an imagination box.'

Eisenstone was frowning. He shook his head. 'I . . . No . . . No, I don't believe . . .'

'Of course, sorry, it's not called that. *I* named it.'

'You named what now?'

'The thought-directed atomic construction device,' Tim said. 'TDACD for short. It's a stupid name.'

The professor's eyes bulged wide behind his glasses. 'I . . . I'm afraid I don't know what you're talking about.'

'Oh,' Dee said, standing. 'Well, what a therapeutic exercise this has been. Sorry, Granddad, we'll leave now.'

'No,' Tim said, holding a hand up to her and staring into Eisenstone's eyes. Tim could read him like a book. He was lying. 'You know perfectly well what the TDACD is – you've been working on it. I bet that's what you were doing before we arrived.' Tim pointed to the goggles on the professor's head. 'Let me guess, it's all theory? You've never successfully used it? Am I right?'

'Young boy, you have a very vivid imagination, but I, I, I—'

'Eisenstone,' Tim whispered, not blinking, not moving even an inch. 'I. Can. Make. It. Work.'

There was a long pause in which the mood shifted. The professor removed his glasses and rubbed his temples. Tim looked to Dee – she was waiting patiently, her head tilted in expectation. Her distrust seemed to be aimed now at her grandfather.

Eventually Eisenstone put his specs back on. 'No one, and I mean *no one*, knows about the TDACD,' he said. 'Indeed, I've not even committed notes to a computer.'

Dee seemed bewildered. 'You really made that machine? It's not ... Granddad, just on scientific grounds, in your wildest dreams, is an alternate universe, as Tim has described, even possible?'

The professor stared into space for a while, shaking his head, but then said, 'Yes. It is possible.'

'Yeah, la, la, la, faster.' Tim did a few circles in the air with his slack hand. 'We're beyond that. It's possible. It's happened.'

Dee regarded Tim out of the corner of her eye. 'Having Granddad say it's theoretically possible that you're not *mental* is not proof of anything.'

'I know, of course it isn't. Eisenstone, go and get the prototype. The TDACD.'

The professor was still flabbergasted but, after a minute or so, he disappeared and returned with the machine.

There it was. The original imagination box, sitting on the table in front of Tim. It was so reassuringly familiar. It was the first thing in this universe that looked perfect, just like he remembered it. All the little exposed transistors were there, like shiny sweets, with the flashing blue light and the round green button. Oh, and the reader, the silly reader with its

84

ridiculously messy bundle of wires. Tim must have had a huge grin because his cheeks began to ache.

'You *do* look like you've seen it before,' Eisenstone said and, instead of doubt, there was hope in his voice.

'Moment of truth,' Dee added.

'In preliminary tests, I've been trying to picture the atomic structures of hydrogen or helium.' The professor stepped towards the table. 'Indeed, the simpler elements. Now, now, you need to place this part on, on your head – this bit is called a *reader*.'

'I know what it all is,' Tim said. 'Reader on noggin, think of what I want, press button, fizz, bang, jiggle, done.'

Confident and excited, Tim pulled the device along the coffee table right up to his knees. He put the reader on his head, closed his eyes and pictured exactly what he wanted. It was crucial he got this creation right, so he spent a moment imagining the finer details. Tim reached out with his index finger and, with a deep breath, pressed the button.

When the gadget beeped and the blue light flashed,

signalling that it had received and downloaded the image, he pulled the reader from his head and slouched back on the sofa, sighing with relief.

The contraption was vibrating around on the table now, with all its mad clunks and shuffles, like an old printer that's on its way out. But for Tim it was music to his ears. It sounded beautiful, a perfect chorus in a perfect song – truly a work of art. And that smell, that lovely lick of steam that curls up out of the back vent. He leant forwards and sniffed – warm electric and plastic and *success*.

Eisenstone was already standing, thrilled just at seeing the prototype working. He hadn't even seen what Tim had created and already it seemed as though he believed every word he'd heard.

'It ... indeed ... it must have been a viable reading. Now ... now what were you thinking about when you pressed the button?' The professor was turning pages over in his notebook, getting ready to document this moment. His hands were trembling.

'Oh, this and that,' Tim said. Dee leant over, pulled open the lock and the hatch flung up.

There was a pause, a horrible moment of silence and doubt. But then:

Phil leapt out and on to the box, spreading his tiny arms to greet them. 'Hello!' the finger monkey sang – his voice was perfect, exactly as Tim imagined.

'Mainly that,' Tim added.

Eisenstone dropped his pen. It clattered on the table, then rolled off and on to the carpet.

'How did you ...' Dee began, sitting back down and leaning in close, fascinated by the creature. 'How on *earth* ...'

'How's it going, Phil?' Tim said.

'Yes, quite all right.' The monkey sat on the edge of the imagination box, his tiny feet dangling.

'So, you've just been recreated,' Tim explained. 'We're sort of in a different universe now.'

'Oh, jolly good. I must say though, I am parched. I fancy blended bananas with ice cream – this universe has bananas and ice cream, I trust? For the love of all things proper, it had better.'

Tim had pictured the precise details of Phil's fur, those large cautious eyes, tiny hands, the memories and, somehow, all those words he didn't even know. But, still, he was half-surprised and fully relieved to see that Phil was as he remembered him, a neat copy from their previous universe.

'I think I saw a banana earlier,' Tim said.

Dee and Eisenstone were frozen rigid in astonishment. After all, they'd been thrown in at the deep end here. Only a minute ago the professor didn't even know his prototype worked at all, now talking finger monkeys were coming out of it.

'Timothy, I invite you to observe my tail,' the monkey said, pulling it round and on to his lap.

'Yeah, I've seen it, congrats.'

'No, look, the stripes – they are odd.'

Sure enough, Tim saw that the fur was kind of zigzagged in pattern – brown and sand-coloured hair splodged messily, instead of being neatly striped. 'Hmm,' Tim said. 'Sorry, I did my best to make you exactly as before.'

'Worry not. I think I prefer it this way anyhow. Hang on, a new universe you say?' Phil asked, his finger on his chin, his eyes wandering around the room. 'At a glance it seems to boast sufficient verisimilitude. Any anomalies? Pertinent differences?'

'Loads,' Tim said. 'You didn't exist until a minute ago.'

'Of course.'

'And I woke up at Glassbridge Orphanage.'

'*No.*'

'Yeah, ran straight home. Elisa didn't recognise me. Bedroom is different, all redecorated, just like a normal hotel room.'

'Get out.'

'I promise.'

'My drawer?'

'Gone, empty. There's no trace that we ever lived there.'

'This is outrageous,' Phil added. 'But it does sound uncannily familiar too. Am I right in presuming our mutual acquaintance Rick Harris was – how can we put this politely – being somewhat liberal with his dispensation of honesty?'

'Yeah, I'm *guessing* he built the imagination station after all.'

'The dastardly rascal.'

'And I think Clarice Crowfield, of all people, somehow got hold of it,' Tim said. 'Get this: she's the Prime Minister now.'

'Goodness. I would submit surprise,' Phil said. 'But also, although wary of coming across vainglorious, I draw your attention to my recommendation of caution, clearly articulated at this machine's speculative conception. I hate to say I told you so, however, I *did* tell you so.'

'I agreed if you remember.'

'Yes, that's right.'

'Anyway, you guys believe me now?' Tim said, looking back up at Eisenstone and Dee, either side of the coffee table. All eyes were still locked silently on the mini monkey. However, the professor slowly nodded.

Turning full circle on top of the box, Phil addressed them all. 'Oh, but this cloud does have a most wondrous lining of silver: the team is back together again. Just *look* at us.' He stopped and spoke to Tim directly, his little fists balled up with excitement.

'What is the plan then, Timothy? Dare I say, some sort of adventure? Oh, Jaffa cakes and whisky – will there be explosions? Tell me there will be explosions.'

'I dunno.' Tim shrugged. 'Maybe.'

Phil straightened his face, then frowned. '"Maybe" doth butter no bacon, Timothy, I need specifics,' he said. 'Run me through the scheme.'

'Well, it's obvious isn't it,' Tim said, glancing at everyone. 'We're going to have to steal the imagination station from Clarice and fix all of this.'

'Heavens,' the monkey said, with a maniac smile. 'Where does one start?'

Chapter 7

'This looks like the place,' Eisenstone said, pulling in and driving between two huge, chain-link gates which slid and rattled open on little wheels. A security guard stepped from a small outbuilding and waved them in – he pointed towards a car park and then said something into the radio clipped on his chest.

The professor drove his quiet, electric car into a space on the far side, beneath a wonky tree – it stood alone, its bushy top shaking in the salty winds. Beyond it Tim could see the sea. It had taken a while to convince Dee and Eisenstone to come here. After all, a prison seemed, at least for them, a strange place to start the investigation. But Tim needed answers. And an inmate here, an old foe, might just have some.

As they approached the entrance to this wide building, Tim took in the tall fences with curled rows of razor wire running around the perimeter, watchtowers with searchlights and armed guards on patrol. Blackbirds with black eyes shuffled and pecked high up on the edge of a nearby concrete wall – below them, CCTV cameras surveyed the lands. Hawk Peak, the professor explained, was the highest-security prison in the country, maybe the world. Tim felt a swell in his chest – a little blip of anxiety at the thought of being locked up in this place. And then he felt another, twice the strength, when he considered that he was already trapped in a far larger and far more disturbing prison.

'Just, just let *me* do the talking,' Eisenstone said as they went in through the front doors.

The previous afternoon, after Tim had recreated Phil and convinced Dee and Eisenstone to take him seriously, they'd all sat in the professor's living room, where they'd had a philosophical conversation about the nature of reality. The old man had spent most of it pacing and wildly gesturing with enthusiasm.

'So, none of this is real?' Dee asked, glancing around. She picked up a cushion and squeezed it, then banged on the coffee table. 'It's all someone else's imagination?'

'It's as real as anything I've created,' Tim said.

'Exhibit A.' Phil presented himself, with a bow.

'Yes. Well, I, I suppose it is no more or less real than any other reality,' Eisenstone said. 'Indeed, there is a school of thought that suggests many worlds exist concurrently. The many worlds theory, in fact. It relates to the nature of very small things. Stuff gets *pretty strange* at an atomic level. It's a bit like … a bit like, oh, yes, yes, have any of you heard of Schrödinger's cat?'

'Rings bells,' Dee said.

'Indeed, the idea goes like this: you put a cat in a sealed box along with some poison which activates randomly.'

'Seems unfair on the cat,' Phil said. The monkey had been sitting on the arm of the sofa, by Tim's side.

'It's a thought experiment,' Eisenstone added. 'We don't actually need a cat for it. Now, now, we wait a bit and, then, indeed, ask, is the cat alive or is the cat dead? It is quite impossible to know. We won't know *for sure* until we look inside, correct?'

Tim nodded. 'If we can't see it or hear it, yeah, we'd have to open the box to be certain.'

'So, therefore, quantum mechanics dictates that the cat is both alive *and* dead at the same time. Only when we open the lid and *look* inside, only when it is *observed*, does reality pick either alive or dead.'

'Cool,' Dee said.

'If a tree falls in the woods, and no one is there to hear it, does it make a sound?' Phil added.

'Yes, yes.' The professor pointed at the monkey. 'Indeed. It is a little like that. Some theorists believe when you flip a coin, the universe splits in two – in one it's heads, in another it's tails. Every choice, every variation, is a fork in the road. A great tree of endless possibility.' Eisenstone paused, then stared at the wall. It seemed he was now talking only to himself. 'Maybe consciousness is the key . . . Maybe reality isn't a physical space which we live in, but rather we are simply isolated minds in a theatre of our own making.

Each brain, each conscious creature is, in a sense, a universe in itself.'

Tim and Dee exchanged a look, eyebrows lifted high.

'What does this hypothetical feline torture, intriguing though it is, have to do with our current predicament?' Phil asked.

Eisenstone blinked and seemed back in the room. 'Well, well, perhaps *everything* exists in all its possible hazy states, all at once – but on a large scale, or, rather, an infinite scale. And the imagination station allows the user to pick which reality we end up in.'

'This is making me go cross-eyed,' Tim said. 'I like talking about consciousness and the universe, but I don't quite understand either.'

'Don't worry,' Eisenstone said. 'No one does.'

As they continued discussing this topic, Dee was sitting cross-legged on the armchair typing away on her granddad's laptop. She hadn't explained what she was doing but, after around ten minutes of keyboard clatter, she lifted her head and laughed.

'Wow,' she said. 'You guys should read this.'

Tim stood and perched on the arm of the chair. Phil scurried on to the laptop, kneeling next to the mouse mat. Tim saw the screen reflected in the monkey's brown eyes – they were so dark and clear he reckoned if he had a magnifying glass he could probably read the website in them.

'I thought I'd look online for similar theories about what Tim was saying,' Dee explained. 'I found this paper written by a psychiatrist. She's been treating a patient who has "elaborate and complex delusions about Clarice Crowfield".' Dee did bunny ears with her fingers. 'A lot of it sounds the same as your story.'

'What's the doctor's name?' Tim asked.

'Joanne Reed. Heard of her?'

'Nope,' Tim said. 'And the patient?'

'He's a convicted criminal – it says he's locked up in Hawk Peak Prison. His name is … let me see … Fredric Wilde.'

'Ding dong,' Phil said.

'You mentioned him earlier,' Dee added. 'The wrong'un who framed Granddad and had a network of mind-control devices.'

Either, Dee then summarised, this indicated that there was some truth in Tim's claims, or it was simply a remarkable coincidence that two people had identical delusions. Both options, she said, were interesting.

Tim decided, as he and Fredric Wilde seemed to be the only people on earth who knew the truth, that they needed to meet up. However, actually having a face-to-face conversation with someone locked up in Hawk Peak was, Eisenstone said, quite tricky.

'You can't, well, you can't just go waltzing into prisons like this one. We'd need fake IDs or something,' he suggested. 'An official letter from a judge or doctor or similar. We'd need it to be co-signed by his lawyer. Even if it was possible, which I stress it isn't, it'd take weeks to arrange.'

Tim had already put the imagination box reader on his head and pressed the button. 'Something like these?' he said, pulling the freshly cooked paperwork from the device.

Now they were all walking down a narrow corridor having been checked and scanned and searched and quizzed about why they wanted to visit Fredric

Wilde. All apart from Phil, who agreed to wait in the car – they were trying not to attract any unwanted attention, after all. He was given the token task of guarding the imagination box prototype, safely stowed away in Eisenstone's car boot. The professor made up a story, said they were distant relatives and had permission from a judge. At reception he handed over forged IDs and letters, which were thoroughly inspected. Tim had a familiar wave of panic, worrying that he might have accidently imagined a mistake on the papers.

Luckily, however, they were allowed to enter.

'So this guy, why *did* he invent mind-control phones?' Dee whispered as they walked.

'Because he was worried about the imagination technology,' Tim explained. 'He was a high-flying business man, a billionaire. He was scared that if everyone had an imagination box, no one would buy anything any more. Money would become worthless. He said society would crumble.'

'Yes, yes,' Eisenstone added. 'The device could well harm commerce and industry.'

'But, you said *we* stopped him?' Dee asked. 'How?'

Even now, after all she'd seen, there was some doubt in Dee's voice – she still didn't fully believe everything.

'It's a long story,' Tim said. 'But in a nutshell: bear-sharks.'

As they entered the final corridor, they went through some more scanners. This one was huge, like a tunnel – a complicated-looking gizmo whizzed round on rails and fired a network of lasers down on to them.

Eventually, however, they arrived at Fredric's cell.

The first thing that Tim noticed, on the back wall, was a large white sign. It had a black clef with a red line running through it. 'No music,' the sign read in bold letters. Tim thought that was a strange and mean rule to have.

And behind, above, he saw a CCTV camera looking right at him. He turned back to the cell.

Fredric was just as Tim remembered, besides seeming much older. He was wearing a baggy grey jumper and jogging bottoms – there were large shadows under his eyes and scruffy stubble on his cheeks. Earlier Tim had been worried about seeing him again, but Fredric was more a sad figure now, rather than a scary one. In fact, the guy was a mess.

However, he still managed a smile. 'Now, of all the people I expected to see …' he said in his thick American accent.

Tim asked how he was, but Fredric just shook his head.

'We … we read that you remember what happened?' Tim said.

There was a long pause – Fredric hesitated and couldn't find the right words.

'Do … do you know the truth too?' he finally said, his eyes wide with hope. 'About Clarice, about everything?'

Tim nodded.

'God, my God,' Fredric said. 'So TRAD actually built the imagination station?'

'How do you know about it?' Dee asked.

'I *used* to have limited access to the Internet,' Fredric said. 'I was reading papers, in all kinds of scientific journals – the agency adopted a policy of transparency after what happened. TRAD's resident neuroscience geek, Rick Harris – he was writing about it. I said this technology is *bad news* ... But I figured he'd never make it work, even if he *did* build it. I mean, they'd need to have abilities like yours for a start ...'

Tim squirmed. 'I ... I kinda ... I made him an exact copy of my brain. I think he used that, like a relay. Sort of transmitted his thoughts through it. I guess that's how it works.'

'Oh, good job,' Fredric said, with very obvious sarcasm. 'I'm relieved though. I've been having therapy.' Sighing, he shook his head again. 'I thought I was crazy.'

'You are crazy,' Tim said. 'Remember all the murders and mind control?'

'No, I mean, like, besides that. Like crazy-crazy. Man, though, it's rad that I was right. So, what's the plan? Is this a jailbreak?' He smiled.

'Well, no,' Tim said.

'Pretty impossible anyway. You know they score prisons by how secure they are?' Fredric stroked the concrete wall then dinged his knuckle on the metal bars that separated them. 'Hawk Peak comes out on top. I think I'm here for the long haul – no matter which reality we're in. So, what *are* you doing here?'

'I just wanted to understand how, or why, *you* can remember everything?' Tim said.

'I think it's a punishment.' Fredric sat on his low bed. 'A while back, in the old universe this is, Stephen Crowfield came to visit me.'

Tim had always felt sorry for Stephen – he was a victim of his mother. Clarice blamed her son for all of *her* failings and used him as a pawn in her schemes. It made Tim sigh to think that she was doing it all over again.

'Why?' he asked. 'What did Stephen want?'

'Well, ya know, his mother was back from the dead,' Fredric said. 'Teleported back into the world. Anyway, she was angry and ambitious as always. I figured the Crowfields read about the imagination station too? Maybe they guessed it wasn't just theory.'

'So, she stole it,' Tim said – he'd already thought as much. 'But what did Stephen want from you?'

'The Nevada facility. That place was quarantined after the incidents, after you guys destroyed it. They wanted access codes to get inside.'

'Why?'

'There were still some teleportation spheres there.' These were like little metal golf balls – if you press the button on an orange one, you will teleport to wherever the blue one is and vice versa. They were one of Wilde Tech Inc's better inventions. 'Point is, an odd number were recovered,' Fredric added. 'Some orange ones were there, buried underground in the dirt, and at least one of their blue counterparts—'

'Was in the Diamond Building,' Tim said, nodding.

'Exactly. And as you know, breaking into TRAD's headquarters ain't easy.'

'So, hang on, this is *your* fault?' Tim asked.

'No, God no.' Fredric stood up. 'I told Stephen to get lost. I ain't gonna go giving them access to my facility. You know me, Tim, you *know* I ain't a fan of all this imagination technology. It's dangerous. Even more dangerous than I ever feared. Just look what it's done. Just look what *you've* done.' Fredric glared at

Tim and then at Eisenstone. The professor glanced at his feet and nodded silently to himself.

'Hey, be reasonable,' Tim said. 'We couldn't have predicted *this*.'

'You helped build a device that can change the universe and you're *surprised* that the universe has changed?' Fredric clapped slowly. 'Ten points to the brainy bunch.'

Now he said it like that, Tim did feel a smidge responsible. Eisenstone too looked pale. The old professor had had a fairly overwhelming twenty-four hours, after all.

'But . . . my defiance came at a cost.' Fredric turned to the wall and pointed at the sign. 'I told Stephen all I had left was music. It was all I could enjoy in here. So when Clarice used the imagination station, she took it away. Hell doesn't roar ya know, it's completely silent. Now go. The game's over, kid. You've lost.'

Chapter 8

They left Hawk Peak Prison having confirmed many of Tim's suspicions. On the way out, they passed a woman wearing a brown suit and thin wire glasses. Tim read her name tag: Doctor Reed – this was Fredric's psychiatrist. And she was watching them intensely as they left, almost like she recognised them. Tim checked over his shoulder as the glass front door closed behind – the doctor, still staring, was making a phone call now.

On the drive back, Dee was sitting in the front seat recalling everything she'd heard and, while maybe she believed Tim now, she still didn't seem interested in his plan. 'In fact, I'm just going to bow out of this one,' she said. 'You guys can go on your crazy adventure if you want. I promise I'll keep it secret.'

'We've got to stop Clarice,' Tim said from the back seat. 'Don't you understand?'

'Why though?' Dee said, shrugging. 'Literally why bother? Just get on with your life. It's all fine.'

'Because . . . because she's . . . she's bad,' Tim said.

Although he hadn't explained it in the best words, this was undeniably true. Clarice *was* bad. Tim had seen recordings of Stephen's childhood memories – he had seen the cruel ways Clarice used to torment her own son. As if that wasn't enough, Tim had also seen inside *her* mind when she transmitted her thoughts through his. Her huge imagination box confirmed it. It created exactly what was inside her: a monster. 'A physical manifestation of everything she was,' Phil had noted in his comic.

'Is she though?' Dee said. 'She used to be, but everything is different now.'

This was a good point, Tim reasoned. 'So . . . what kind of prime minister is she?'

'I gather everyone loves her,' Dee said.

'Indeed, she does receive a lot of praise,' Eisenstone added, still concentrating on the road.

'Even that's weird – people are meant to hate politicians,' Tim said. 'This is just because that's how she's imagined it. Trust me, she's not good.'

'Well, I've heard no complaints,' Dee said. 'Everyone always gets into the spirit on Crowfield Day, wearing wigs and that.'

'What the hell is Crowfield Day?' Tim asked, frowning.

'You know, it's Crowfield Day. It's … it's like … it's a bit like Christmas, but better.'

'Better?!'

'My point is this,' Dee said, shuffling round in the front seat and looking directly at him now. 'What makes you think *you* can imagine a better, fairer, more whatever universe than she can?'

'It's not real,' Tim said slowly, growing angry now. 'It's all a lie.'

'One cannot help but wonder how she ascended to such a position in your minds as it were?' Phil said. 'In your somewhat apocryphal memories?'

'The Crowfield family dynasty goes back generations,' the professor explained. 'But Clarice herself, she's been in politics since her twenties – and has always been popular. A little over fifteen years ago, she was elected into office and her first two terms went so well that everyone agreed to keep her on. And, and with no real challengers, there's been no need for any elections.'

This backstory Clarice had written herself made Tim shake his head. He didn't know a great deal about politics and democracy, but he knew that people having a vote was quite an important part of it all.

'So, what, she's just the Prime Minister forever, and everyone's cool with that?' Tim asked.

'A dictatorship is the best system, as long as the dictator is a good one,' Dee said. 'That's what they taught us in school.'

'That is sort of true,' Phil said.

'Whose side are you on?' Tim frowned at the monkey. 'It's not the best system, because who decides what is good and what is bad?'

'You, apparently,' Dee said.

'Look, whatever,' Tim huffed. 'All this doesn't matter because it's *not real*.'

'Well, as Granddad said, it's *as* real as any other reality and it's all we've ever known. So, let's just keep our heads down and make do.'

Luckily for Tim, things were about to become just as problematic for Dee and Eisenstone as they were for him. When they arrived at the professor's house, it was being ransacked. There were two police vans outside, scanner drones (like the one he'd seen in the alleyway) flying around the building, peering in through the windows, and even a helicopter hovering high above. Officers had kicked in the professor's door. There were hundreds of them – one going through the bins, others searching the garden with sniffer dogs, some standing watch with guns pointed to the ground. Their uniforms caught Tim's attention – they were all wearing identical grey body armour and dark grey helmets, with visors. They looked as much like soldiers as policemen.

'Oh ... dear,' Eisenstone said. 'What's all this?'

Instead of stopping at his house, alarmed by what he'd seen, the professor simply kept driving, off up the street and then round the corner. They parked in the basement floor of a quiet multistorey car park. It was comparatively dark in here and, although there was no visible water, somehow damp.

'Why were they trashing your house?' Tim wondered.

They could still hear the helicopter somewhere out there, rumbling and thumping like a thousand drums.

'Well, we have used some forged documents . . . but, but that isn't bad enough to raid my house, surely.'

'I dunno,' Tim started. 'Maybe—'

'Uh oh, this is not good,' Dee said, peering down at her phone.

She held it up for Tim and Eisenstone to see. On the screen was a news website and the lead story's headline simply read, 'WANTED' in big letters.

Below that was, 'UK police issue nationwide arrest warrant for dangerous fugitives.'

And below that there were three photographs. One of Eisenstone's face. One of Dee's face. And one of Tim's face.

'Hey,' Phil said, pouting and frowning. 'What about me?'

'All right, what the hell is going on?' Tim said after a short silence.

'It's all your fault,' Dee said, shaking her head. 'Everything was just fine until you turned up. Now we're wanted? Those were *Grey Guards* back there you know. They're not messing about.'

'Grey Guards?' Tim asked. 'Who are they?'

'Really? You don't know?' Dee said. She sounded surprised, almost as though he was being stupid.

'I'm from an alternate reality – give me a break.'

'The Grey Guards are basically . . .' She thought for a moment. 'They're like the most serious police. They have guns and they do all sorts of secret shady stuff, all over the world. Keep everything in order. If they're after you then, well, let's say you are in *big* trouble.'

'Oh … I see. And they're called Grey Guards because of the uniform?'

'That, and they're all clones of a bloke called Dennis Grey,' Dee said. 'Think he was a war hero or something. He's basically rock hard and really clever. Perfect blueprint.'

Tim scrunched his eyes and rubbed them with his

thumb and finger. 'Clones?' He sighed.

'Yeah. You *don't* have an elite police force made up of clones in your universe?'

Tim slowly shook his head. However, not for the first time, he found himself genuinely curious about this world. It made sense, he thought, for Clarice to have an army of obedient officers she could send to do her bidding.

'Can you think how and why they tracked us so quickly?' the professor asked.

'I suppose, if someone … Oh,' Tim said, remembering what he'd seen as they left Hawk Peak Prison. 'The doctor? Fredric's psychiatrist – she was phoning someone as we left. Reporting us maybe?'

'But, but why would *she* care?' Eisenstone said.

'Of course.' Tim sighed. 'They were probably on the lookout for us.'

'Why?'

'Think about it,' Tim explained. 'I bet Clarice ensured that the doctor would let her know if anyone made contact with Fredric, and we did. So, now she knows that we're on to her.'

'Surely that's a big problem?' Dee said.

But Tim was oddly relieved by this turn of events. 'At least now we're in the same boat,' he said.

'I *still* haven't done anything wrong,' Dee added. 'I'm gonna turn myself in and—'

'No,' Tim interrupted her. 'You can't. None of us can. This woman is dangerous. Just *think* what she would do to keep her secret.'

Phil was standing on the middle seat in the back of the car, looking left and right as they argued – it seemed he was enjoying the conversation.

'Oh, great,' Dee said. 'So now the most powerful woman in the country – sorry, the world – is going to *kill* us because of what we know? This is just perfect, this is just— Why is your monkey smiling?'

'Rainbows and dog eggs,' Phil exclaimed, placing his tiny hand on his tiny chest. 'I meant no offence. However, yes, your eyes deceive you not – I am taking no small portion of delight from this.'

'Why?' Dee said.

'Yeah, why?' Tim added. 'Seriously, Phil, you've misjudged this whole thing – this is bad.'

'Oh, Timothy, do not project your solemn worries on to me,' the monkey said. 'Think how enriched this experience will make us – what inspiration and nostalgia we shall feel in our hearts, in our *souls*.'

'Are you not even a little bit concerned?' Tim asked.

'We have wiggled out of worse predicaments.'

'No, Phil,' Tim said. 'No, we haven't.'

Having fully agreed that this really was problematic on an almost unthinkably large scale, Dee turned the conversation in the right direction.

'Fine, it's done, this is the situation,' she said. 'So, how can we fix it?'

'I submit that we need somewhere to lie low,' Phil suggested. 'Somewhere familiar, and yet most inconspicuous.' He stepped to the car door and peered up out of the window, towards the sky. 'How far away is the moon?'

'Too far,' Dee said.

'It's a good idea though,' Tim added. 'Not the moon thing, that's insane, but hiding out somewhere. And I think I know just the place.'

Chapter 9

Tim instructed Eisenstone to drive across town. As he pulled away, the monkey wobbled, lost his balance and fell flat on the middle car seat, then literally bounced into the air as the wheels rode over the peak of the exit ramp.

On the way, they all switched off their mobile phones, in case they were traced. Another reason was that Dee's mum, having seen the news, was understandably concerned and kept ringing, despite her daughter's attempts at explaining.

'I'll probably be home later,' Dee told her mother. 'I'm safe, I'm with Granddad, this is all just a big misunderstanding.'

Tim thought of Elisa and felt a sudden sadness – she

would have called, if only she knew who he was.

After a short drive they turned into a back alley, about a mile or so from the Dawn Star Hotel, and parked up near a large bin. They all clambered from the car – this seemed a reasonable place to ditch it. The professor retrieved the imagination box and slammed the boot shut.

'Got everything?' he said, a few pieces of litter rolling at his feet in the breeze. Strange crisp packets with strange logos – again, Tim felt like he was on holiday.

Dee nodded, but Tim was distracted by a weed growing through a crack in the tarmac. It had a bright red flower, with yellow thorns up the stalk and tiny blue berries between the petals – so blue and glassy they looked like mini marbles. He had never seen anything like it before. Had Clarice created new plant life too? Standing upright, Tim turned back to the car.

'Light bulb. Ding. Maybe,' Phil said, his arms and head dangling from Tim's top pocket, '*maybe* we ought to burn it?'

'Burn what?' Eisenstone asked. 'Burn, burn the car you mean? No, no, no.'

'If the authorities find it they will know we are close,' Phil explained. 'If we are adopting the habits of felons, it seems most apt to go the, shall we say, full pig.'

'Hog,' Tim corrected him.

'Quite,' the monkey nodded. 'Full hog pig.'

'He's right,' Dee said. 'People *do* do that when they're on the run.'

Tim could feel Phil against his chest, warm and wriggling with excitement – the monkey glanced back up to Eisenstone and blinked. 'Please?'

'I, well, I haven't even got a lighter.'

A moment later Tim was crouching behind the bin, wearing the imagination box reader. Hidden in a slightly larger cardboard box, the machine shuffled about on the alleyway floor – a ribbon of steam and the flashing blue light and it was done. From inside Eisenstone took a small bottle of petrol and a box of matches – each one was a different length and each head had a wonky red lump bulging on top. Tim said he rushed the creation – that's why it was odd. But this was the second thing he'd made with accidental imperfections, just like Phil's tail. Were his skills simply rusty, he wondered, or was it the chip in his neck interfering with his mind? At any rate, he would remember to concentrate hard from now on.

After expressing a few more doubts – as most decent adults would – the professor agreed with the plan. He told them all to stand well back and then doused the seats with the fluid, stepped a few paces away and struck one of the longer matches.

'It all smells wonderful,' Phil said.

'Actually,' Dee whispered to Tim. 'Burning it will probably attract more attention – it makes more sense just to replace the number plates.'

'I thought that straight away,' Tim said. 'But I kind of want to do this option now.'

'I concur,' Phil added.

'To be fair, me too,' Dee said.

A flat line of orange and blue flame crept along the tarmac, up the car's door, over the window and – with a *whoomphf* of bass – erupted inside. As it burned, Phil made a frame with his fingers and thumbs and said he would like to draw the image. However, if he had to choose, Tim would have drawn that flower.

He'd seen fire plenty of times before, but that plant was brand new. Generally, he preferred to draw things from his imagination, things which didn't exist. And here was something both real and not real. The ultimate subject for a picture.

Sadly they didn't have time to stick around to draw or toast marshmallows, so they took a few backstreets and tried to stay out of sight. They were particularly careful to avoid the drones which flew and zipped and buzzed about overhead.

'What *are* those things?' Tim asked, squinting up at one of the round, hovering bots.

Dee explained they were Grey Guard drones, which would usually just be out on patrol. But now they were almost certainly searching for them. In one wider alleyway, Tim looked up and counted at least five of the machines, balanced like small planets above the city. It wouldn't be long, he thought, until they found the car.

But, with tactical timing, they managed to stay out of sight of the surveying cameras and, after crossing two more side streets, a large industrial estate and another alleyway, they arrived at the rear car park of the Dawn Star Hotel. Led by Tim, who knew his way around this building instinctively, they crept inside through a back entrance.

'Won't they look for us here?' Dee whispered as they arrived in the quiet hallway.

'Not where we're heading,' Tim said.

He guided them to the stairwell, knowing exactly where to walk to avoid the CCTV cameras, and headed up.

The very highest floor in the Dawn Star Hotel wasn't occupied, at least not by guests. In fact, it was used pretty much only for storage. Some of the rooms were packed, literally up to the door, with furniture and general bits and pieces – extra bedding, rugs, clocks, old mini fridges, boxes filled with cutlery and tablecloths and ornaments and even, in one room, an old bicycle. Most of it wasn't good enough to use but, according to Elisa, was still too good to throw away.

After trying a couple of doors – which Tim accessed with keys he'd quickly imagined, half of which came out as failures, made of things like Play-Doh and sand – they found the ideal room to set up base. Room ninety-eight was the perfect hiding place because it was only *half* filled with clutter. This meant they could get inside and then push all the storage containers and towers of chairs and whatnot right up against the doorway. So to access room ninety-eight you would have to lie down and crawl between the narrow legs of about six or seven stacks of chairs – like navigating a dwarf's dark labyrinth. And, in the middle of the former guest suite, they had turned tables upright and arranged them like a line of screens, with one extra propped up against the window. If anyone came looking for them up here, they would be met with a seemingly solid wall of stuff and would assume the room was full to capacity.

When they had finished, Tim squeezed in, crawled carefully on his stomach like a soldier through wooden chair legs, reached up, and locked the door behind them, then he shuffled back the way he came. He even blocked the tunnel with a plastic container filled with paperwork.

'There,' he said, as he heaved himself out and stood up straight. 'We're safe now.' He brushed a dusty cobweb from his shirtsleeve, then wiggled the cartilage in his nose to keep from sneezing.

'What a fabulous little den,' Phil said.

It was good, Tim thought, because if the Grey Guards had asked Elisa if she had seen him, she would have said yes – but then she would have told them that he'd run away from the hotel.

'It is definitely … well, I suppose, cosy?' the professor added. 'Cosy indeed.'

'Yep.' Tim nodded. 'En-suite bathroom is through there.' He pointed to the door. 'We have everything we need in here.'

Creasing up her top lip, Dee looked around the remaining patch of thin carpet. 'Apart from food, water, beds, soap, clean clothes, entertainment and a long list of other things,' she said.

Tim rolled his eyes, then tore the cardboard exterior away from the imagination box prototype. 'You guys still really haven't grasped what this thing can do,' he said.

Sitting cross-legged on the floor, Tim, Dee, Eisenstone and Phil surrounded the contraption as though it was a campfire. It was being regarded, quite rightly, as their lifeline. A circuit board on the side was loose from transporting it, so the professor tightened some screws with a coin then used a bit of tape and an elastic band to hold it in place. Of course Tim knew it was a remarkable piece of technology, but seeing Eisenstone tweak it with such basic methods made him appreciate it all over again. He'd often taken it all for granted but, when he stopped to think, it really was amazing what human hands could build.

Finally, the machine whirred back into life – all the little lights, the gentle electric humming of infinite potential.

'So, what do you guys want?' Tim asked, placing the reader on his head.

Half an hour later, the small space had been completely transformed. Tim created fabric beanbags for them all, which he then filled with stuffing. He made three thick runner rugs which he rolled out on the floor. Then countless cushions and pillows of all shapes and sizes and, for some reason, a teddy bear (he just had soft things in his mind and got carried away). A lot of the new furniture had to be assembled, such is the challenge of using an imagination box only a little larger than a microwave. Another innovative method saw them tilting the contraption on its side and holding the lid open while Tim imagined a tall lamp. With careful pacing, Dee and the professor pulled the full length out – like retrieving impossible items from a magician's hat.

Everything, like everything else he'd made, had little faults and charms. Imperfections here, angles not quite right there, the odd kink in the rug or error in a pattern.

But still, it *was* cosy, snug and, put simply, the most comfortable place Tim could imagine. Lit by candles with light so warm and multicoloured they would be better set in a fantasy. In fact the scene was, as Phil put it, 'So ineffably beautiful that should you take a photograph, it would look like a dream spoken in the language of paint and few would believe it was real.'

They ate dinner of their choices: Eisenstone went for a traditional roast with all the trimmings, Dee enjoyed a bowl of steaming noodles which were dark with soy sauce and made a bed for sweet and sour chicken, while Tim kept it simple with a cheeseburger and fries. The monkey, who often behaved as you would expect a monkey to behave, took great pleasure in his tiny banana milkshake.

'I am also partial to climbing the occasional tree,' Phil said, stirring with his straw.

After this, Tim set up a little kitchen area in the corner, where he made them all tea (this was easier than creating multiple cups and teapots). He was holding a full teacup, balanced on a saucer, when the discussion turned – as it had done a lot over the last day – to the implications of imagining a new universe.

'What strikes me is all the things that are the same,' Tim said.

'Indeed, I, I suppose it is the status quo unless imagined otherwise?' Eisenstone suggested.

'Maybe,' Tim said, sipping from his tea. 'That would make sense. Anyway, does anyone want dessert?'

'High time we conjured up some chocolate,' Phil said.

'Top idea,' Tim agreed, lifting his teacup.

'What the hell is *chocolate*?' Dee asked.

Gasping, Tim dropped the cup and saucer he was holding, which shattered at his feet.

'Clarice really has created a nightmare,' the monkey added, staring at the wall. 'We must unravel this madness, post haste.'

Within ten minutes they were all lying, spreadeagled, on their own beanbags (Phil on his miniature one), lips and fingers still sticky, groaning and sighing. Some of the combinations Tim made tasted so good that he thought about going into business – toffee, dark, milk, white, raisins, caramel, nuts real and imagined, all arranged in incredible ways. And it proved, above all, the perfect way to introduce these poor souls to the delicious world of chocolate.

Room ninety-eight soon felt like a true sanctuary – it seemed as though the world's problems not only couldn't get them in here, but simply did not exist outside these walls. As though if you were to zoom out and out and far away, you would view the room aglow in a black abyss of nothing – an oasis in an endless void, like something created for a computer game.

As Tim slumped lower and fell asleep, he had an image

in his mind of sliding through the bricks and finding himself outside in this blank space and falling and falling and watching their beautiful den in room ninety-eight drift away above until it was a single pixel. Like a star. This jolted him and he opened his eyes. He thought of Elisa – she was probably just a few metres below. He wondered what she might be doing at that moment. Cleaning up, getting ready for bed herself maybe. Or maybe she was already asleep. Did *this* Elisa dream of having a child? Did she miss him, even though she didn't know him?

He smiled at the flickering candle nearby and closed his eyes. It was nearly perfect, he thought as he drifted off again, if only Elisa would be herself.

In fact, he realised, beating Clarice and putting things right wasn't the main reason he was so driven. Really, Tim just wanted things back to how they were between him and ... and his mum. The word felt natural now. If he could have that, he'd accept defeat and let Clarice Crowfield have everything else.

Tim woke sometime around sunrise, which was little
e than a faint glow on the edge of the table they

had pressed against the window. Dee was sitting, wrapped in a blanket, in the corner, squatting low and watching the small TV Tim had created the previous night. Phil was perched on her shoulder and Eisenstone was by her side.

'What,' Tim said, stretching. 'What you watching?'

'The news.' She turned the TV's volume up a few notches. 'We're on it.'

'... considered armed and dangerous,' the reporter said. 'George Eisenstone is believed to be on the run with his granddaughter Dee and another child, thought to be Timothy Hart.'

The news then flicked to CCTV stills of them walking across the car park of Hawk Peak Prison, then another of them in reception. A final frame popped up on screen – it was of Tim looking at the camera right by Fredric's cell. He remembered the moment well.

'The police think we did it,' Dee said.

'Did what?' Tim asked, turning slightly, scared of the answer.

'Fredric is dead.' Dee sighed. 'And they're saying we murdered him.'

Chapter 10

Tim stared at his own face on the news – then a photograph of Fredric Wilde arrived on screen. Sure enough, the reporter said Eisenstone, Tim and Dee were wanted in connection with his murder.

'I don't understand,' Dee whispered.

'Clarice. She must have ordered it,' Tim said.

'How on earth would we have been able to kill him anyway?' Dee asked.

Previously Tim had thought that if they found a way to *prove* what Clarice had done, they could try and expose her – get it in the newspapers and on the Internet. Let the world know that she was a wrong'un. Now though, that clearly wasn't an option. Who would believe a group of murderers, especially ones with such insane theories about the Prime Minister?

'That doesn't matter,' Tim said to Dee. 'It's far-fetched to accuse us of murdering someone in a prison, but it sounds way more believable than the truth ever will.'

The TV then cut to another familiar face – the multicoloured jumper girl from Glassbridge Orphanage. She was standing outside the building, talking to a reporter – at the bottom of the screen it said she was a 'Close friend of Timothy Hart'.

'He seemed strange that morning,' she said. 'I've known him all my life – you can just tell when something is wrong.'

'It's her,' Tim whispered. 'The megaphone girl.'

'Did he say where he might go?' the reporter asked.

The girl hesitated, then nodded. 'Yes, he said he was leaving Glassbridge and heading ... heading north. But he didn't say why.'

'You told her where you were going?' Dee asked.

'No,' Tim said. 'No, I didn't say ...' And then he realised. 'I think ... I think she's covering for me. The police, the Grey Guards, they must have asked her.

This is good. It'll divert their attention even more. I think, here, she's my best friend?'

Even after everything, the idea that he had a different history muddled his mind in ways he couldn't explain. And still, for reasons he didn't understand *yet*, he couldn't remember any of it – for which he was hugely grateful.

'You said *I* was your best friend,' Dee added. She seemed slightly annoyed.

'You are my best friend.' He caught Phil's eye. 'Best real friend,' Tim added. The monkey stepped to Dee's side and copied her expression, although his was far sassier. 'That was the wrong word,' Tim qualified. 'You know what I mean: best *human* friend.'

'Well, the news is saying *she* is, so …'

'I've never even … I don't know who … I don't even know her name,' Tim said, his voice a little high-pitched. 'You can't be jealous. You've known me for a day. Trust me, you *are* my best friend. She's just some weird creation to make my new life look real.'

Still, he was oddly comforted to know there was *someone* here that was looking out for him.

As Tim created some imperfect breakfast for them all, he remembered a hazy dream he had last night after he'd flown off and out of room ninety-eight in his mind. In the dream Clarice was *his* mother and, in a weird way, *he* was Stephen. It didn't play out in the correct order, but he saw snippets of what Clarice used to do to her son. Shouting at him, hitting him for no reason other than her own anger, her own failures.

And now Fredric Wilde had been added to her ever-growing list of victims.

Tim sat in silence on his beanbag, watching a thin strip of daylight on the rug, and felt a strange sadness. Fredric was no saint but he didn't deserve to die. In fact, despite everything Fredric had done, Tim still thought there was good in him – somewhere, deep down, but it was there. The same could not be said for Clarice Crowfield.

He wished then, from the bottom of his heart, that there was some way they could just stay in room ninety-eight, this safe space, forever. But he knew that too wasn't an option.

'Wait,' Dee said, turning to face him. 'I have a

brilliant idea.' She threw the blanket off her shoulders and stood up. 'I am about to deliver a bombshell,' she said. 'A laser-guided logic rocket. Are you ready?'

Tim nodded. 'Do it.'

'The imagination box – it creates anything you imagine, right?'

'That's a good explanation, yeah.'

'OK,' Dee said, pacing. 'And, as we discussed, the information required to create any of these items, this finger monkey, these wonky croissants and so on … You don't – you can't – personally *know* the atomic make-up of these things.'

Eisenstone was paying close attention to his granddaughter – he'd clearly thought long and hard about how his invention might work. 'That's right,' he said. 'The code, the raw data … the, the blueprints for *any* item created, even tiny ones, would fill thousands of thick, thick books. Tim couldn't – at least consciously – *know* it.'

'Well, then, create a map,' Dee suggested. 'A map with the location of the imagination station marked on it. Actually, for that matter, you *could* just create a booklet containing the solution to every problem you'll ever have.'

'What impact would that have on the already flimsy case for free will?' Phil wondered.

'Or,' Dee went on, 'could you even cut out the middleman and make a new imagination station?'

'I would steer away from that option,' Eisenstone said. 'This technology is powerful, the implications are, well, huge. Grand indeed. Creating conflict between two machines competing for reality? It could well damage the very fabric of space-time. A schizophrenic universe would be no good for anyone. The risk is ... is just too high.'

'Fine, but the map could work?' Dee said. 'We'd need a simple experiment to test it. If you ... maybe ... I know, try and create a piece of paper with Granddad's pin number on it.'

Tim explained that he had previously used the technology in ways which could be considered 'psychic' – like when he'd used his own box to create computer passwords written inside fortune cookies. However, the piece of paper that Eisenstone pulled from the box had three numbers right and one number wrong.

'This, this is still incredible,' the professor said. 'I can't fathom the odds of this being a lucky guess.'

'So, what does that mean?' Dee asked. 'Tim can access *some* information outside of his mind?'

'Hmm.' Eisenstone thought for a moment. 'It is hard to say . . . Perhaps yes, but his own preconceptions, his own knowledge and thoughts and emotions are, are maybe contaminating the process?' He looked at Tim now. 'Or perhaps your abilities are waning with age – you're growing up, which can cause the imagination to fade.'

Tim frowned – he didn't like that idea at all. 'No way,' he said. 'It's gotta be the chip.'

He turned his head so they could look at the scar on his neck. Earlier he had told them what it did, but the professor seemed compelled to ask about it again.

'According to Rick, who made it, it basically interferes with my imagination,' Tim explained. 'It sounds bad but, trust me, it's a good thing. Without it, anything I imagine simply appears. Nice pattern on the wall, cup of tea, cool breeze on a hot day, megaspiders, fire, sabre-toothed tiger. You name it. No need for a box, or a reader. There's no barrier between the real world and my imagination.'

'Sounds awesome,' Dee said.

'It can be,' Tim admitted. 'When I can *control* it. But it can also be extremely dangerous.'

'Indeed,' Eisenstone said. 'Not all thoughts are good thoughts.'

'Exactly.' Tim nodded in agreement. 'Using the box seems a much safer way – I just have to concentrate, that's all. So, if I was to imagine a map . . .'

He closed his eyes and pressed the button, focusing on keeping his mind clear. When the machine finished he pulled out a small booklet, which he folded open and flattened on the floor.

'Where is this?' Dee asked.

Eisenstone put his glasses on and peered down. 'Some of these streets are recognisable.'

It looked like a detailed road map. However at the edges the lines faded away to nothing. And some of them clearly weren't accurate – some numbers and road names were just nonsense, random symbols and letters in strange orders. One lane even curled round and made a face.

However, in the centre was a red X.

'It's London,' Dee said. 'Look, that's the Thames.' She traced the splodgy, blue smear that ran along the map with her finger.

'Then ... then indeed,' the professor nodded, stroking his chin. 'Then this would be Crowfield Tower.'

'She's got her own tower,' Tim said. 'Of course.'

'So ... either the imagination station is *in* the tower, or that's where Tim believes it to be?' Dee said.

'At any rate,' Phil declared, scurrying across the paper. 'I think this is where we should set our sights.' The monkey then began marching clumsily along the map, patting his chest and letting out a quiet roar. 'Timothy, look. I am Ping Pong. No, wait, King Pong.'

'Kong.'

'Kong Pong?'

'Are you OK?' Tim asked.

'It's settled then,' Dee said. 'We need to break into Crowfield Tower.'

Chapter 11

Of course, breaking into Crowfield Tower would not be easy – in fact, the more Tim heard about the building, the more he felt it might be impossible. It seemed to command London, and for him it stood out even more so, being a completely new feature on the familiar skyline. There was the London Eye, Big Ben, the Shard and then, bigger than the lot, this vast skyscraper – a black, one-hundred-and-fifty-storey column.

Dee had pulled up some pictures of the building on her phone (Tim had made them all new ones). There was a photo of the lobby. In the entrance there was a huge shield painted on the marble floor. Across it were three black crows, one on top of the other. It was weirdly familiar – then Tim realised he *had* seen the image before, only a slightly different version. This was England's coat of arms, but the historic three lions had been replaced by three crows, each with spread wings and sharp beaks. Clarice had put her stamp on everything.

Tim asked about how far her reach actually extended and was told that not only was she Prime Minister of the UK, but also many, many other nations.

'Indeed, the Great British Empire?' Eisenstone had said, astonished by Tim's surprise. They still thought all this was normal.

Compelled by Tim's reaction, the professor gave him a brief history lesson, with various photos and videos streaming on Dee's new phone. Iconic twentieth-century pictures of world wars, marching armies, Grey Guards in formation and even space travel. Things he recognised, things he didn't, but all things tainted by the Crowfield family colours and badges. The most striking image was a modified American flag, with three black crows instead of white stars, held by an astronaut during the first moon landing.

'She's … she's rewritten history,' Tim whispered, feeling that now familiar queasy sensation in his stomach.1

They showed Tim a map of the world, with Britain's – or rather Clarice's – territory marked out in grey. So many countries, Tim thought, shaking his head, so much power. And Crowfield Tower was, the professor said, the 'epicentre, the eye of the storm'.

'A heist like this will need some planning,' Tim had said.

It was crucial, for example, to have a more accurate idea of *where* within the building the imagination station would be. Specific details like this were a struggle for Tim to conjure in the box.

With that in mind, Tim, Phil and Dee ventured up to Cedar Woods, on the outskirts of Glassbridge, to gather some intelligence. It was late in the evening, trees loomed tall and dark all around them as night scared dusk away. Nearby creatures shuffled out of sight – an early owl sung somewhere above.

They clambered up a small hill, twigs snapping underfoot, then stepped through some mossy roots and prepared themselves.

The trees, Tim noticed, looked exotic – ever-so-slightly different to how he remembered them in these woods. A bit straighter, a bit bigger, a bit …

'What kind of trees *are* these?' he asked, touching the rough, cold bark and recalling that cool flower he'd seen in the alleyway.

'I dunno.' Dee shrugged. 'Tall ones.'

Tim wiped his hand on his jeans, his thumb sticky with sap, and arched his head to look up through the branches at the half-blue night sky. He turned around slowly, spinning the world. Were the stars slightly brighter too? Or was he just paying more attention now and imagining differences?

Was he forgetting how things should be? The thought stirred some panic in his chest.

'Right,' Dee said, pulling her phone from her pocket and bringing his attention back down to earth. 'Firstly, we need to call the police.'

This was one of those ideas that sounded completely

insane when Dee first explained it. They needed, she said, to hack into the police record system.

'Why?' Tim had asked.

'Because that will have precise information, maps, layouts, the works – it'll tell us everything we need to know about Crowfield Tower. I bet it's got a vault or a safe or something. That's where *I'd* hide a secret device.'

'What do they even *do* in Crowfield Tower?' Tim asked.

'It's like the main government building – they have meetings, all that sort of thing. Make laws.'

'Not dissimilar to the Houses of Parliament?' Phil asked from Tim's top pocket.

'The what?' Dee frowned – another slight tweak to this universe. 'Anyway, it's also where the Crowfield family live.'

It made sense to Tim that Clarice would give herself such a prestigious and dominating home.

'So, yeah,' Dee explained. 'We'll need a security drone. The drones are operated by the Grey Guard mainframe. They are programmed to respond to incidents, film crimes, give feedback to the police and Grey Guards and so on.'

'How does one learn such things?' Phil said.

'It's all online – there're even diagrams. They are connected to the record system – they have to be. So they fly along, scan people's faces and number plates and stuff – *beep, beep, beep* – and if they match with a wanted person, they call it in. Then human police turn up. Or, if they spot *us*, Grey Guards.'

'Makes sense.' Tim nodded

'But, obviously, we can't just hack into the system because it'll shut down – it'll have firewalls and security and all that nonsense. Only people with proper codes can access it. And there are only a certain number of IDs. We need an *official* one. And we can't kidnap a policeman, and certainly not a Grey Guard. So we'll grab a drone, smash it open, plug in a laptop, then use *its* ID to access the records. Bob's ya donkey.'

'You are capable of hacking the software within a police drone?' Phil wondered.

'What? No. But Tim can surely create a laptop with the necessary sort of programming or whatever on it? Right?'

'I'll try . . .'

So here they were, in this rapidly darkening woodland, about to phone the police on themselves. Professor Eisenstone, being the most wanted of them all, stayed in room ninety-eight. As an adult, he stood to lose the most. Dee reasoned that she and Tim could always claim to be victims themselves – tricked into doing all of this. Children, she said, could quite literally get away with murder.

Dee's face and upper body were lit by her mobile. She dialled the three most serious numbers you can dial and pressed call.

'Nine nine nine emergency, which service do you require?' The phone was on loudspeaker. The voice was stern. Tim swallowed and felt a tremble of anxiety. This was definitely illegal.

'Police,' Dee said.

'What is the nature of your emergency?' the voice asked.

'Right, yeah,' Dee began. 'Um, I think I saw someone trying to steal sheep in the fields by Cedar Woods, in Glassbridge.'

'Sheep?' Tim whispered, squinting in confusion.

Dee placed her hand over the mobile's microphone. 'It can't be *too* serious or they'll send proper police, we just need one drone.'

'Sorry, is this a prank call?'

'No, seriously, someone—'

'Young lady, calling the police is a serious matter. This is not a joke—'

'Listen, some nutbag is up here mucking about with sheep – you'll get in trouble if they find out you ignored this call. I know they're recorded.'

The controller sighed. 'Fine, a drone has been dispatched to conduct a sweep of Cedar Woods. But if this turns out to be—'

'Yeah, great, whatever,' Tim said, pressing the red button to hang up. He grabbed his heart, relieved the call was over.

'Now,' Dee said, 'we wait.'

Ten minutes passed and they both ended up sitting,

with their legs dangling, on a large outcrop of rocks they'd found. Phil waited on Tim's knee.

'You think Granddad's all right?' Dee asked.

'He seems pretty overwhelmed about everything.'

'Feels responsible, I guess.'

'I am reminded of Alfred Nobel's fabled and nuanced relationship with his own work,' Phil said.

Tim nodded in agreement. Dee frowned.

'He invented dynamite and thought it would be great for mining,' Tim explained. 'Which it is – it's well good for that sort of thing. But it's also brilliant for killing people. Made old Nobel proper sad.'

'He shouldn't have been surprised – people will always find a way to do bad stuff,' Dee said. 'Even a stick can be a weapon. Hang on, hear that?'

There was a faint buzzing and, beyond the hedgerows, a little red dot lifted and flew smoothly along the line of the field. Halfway up, its searchlight came on – a cone of white spread out in front of it.

'Here we go,' Dee said, rising to her feet. Phil leapt back to Tim's pocket.

Tim had suggested all kinds of innovative ways

to bring the drone down – EMP grenades, net traps, even a bow and arrow (admittedly not the best idea). However Dee had said, with a casual shrug, 'I'm gonna throw a rock at it.'

So that's why, at their feet, they had collected a small pyramid of stones – some wonky flints with nasty angles, some perfectly round tennis-ball-sized ones and even some smaller gravelly types that could jam up its systems.

The metal orb's searchlight sent the tree shadows long into the woods, sweeping across quickly one by one, each like a sundial on fast forward.

'Right, here it comes,' Dee said, rolling the balaclava Tim made earlier down on her face. He did the same. He could only see her mouth and her white eyes. She looked appropriately like a criminal in her leather jacket and black woollen mask.

A vague pulsing noise came around them as the drone approached. When it was about twenty metres away, Dee threw a rock but completely missed.

'Damn.'

However, it seemed to notice and slowed to a

stop, spinning its searchlight – it appeared almost as though it was in a panic.

Tim took two steps forward and threw a cold, weighty stone with all his might. There was a loud, hollow clonk and the drone wiggled, dipped a little, but stayed airborne. Then, as though it just somehow *knew* where they were, its search beam swung round and locked firmly on them both. The glare hurt Tim's eyes, but he shielded his face and threw more rocks.

'Cease your activities at once,' a deep voice echoed from the machine. Tim could hear Dee huffing with each throw. 'Damage to police property is an offence which carries a charge of—'

With a spark, the searchlight disappeared and, somewhere in the fresh dark, there was a heavy, clattering thud as it landed. Tim's vision readjusted to see the drone on the grass. Dee swooped in and knelt by its side. She pulled open the laptop, grabbed the plug and then shook her head at the complicated machine. Tim arrived. Up close it was much larger and more substantial than he'd guessed – there was a desperate, electrical fizz coming from its megaphone and a buckled antenna on top was ticking left to right, sounding like a car's indicator.

'Aw, I kind of feel sorry for it,' Tim said.

However, Dee clearly did not. Without a word she lifted a flint above her head and proceeded to smash the metal casing with repeated blows. Eventually, the thing was silent and its electronic innards exposed. It looked like the inside of a computer – it even had USB plug sockets, which they swiftly connected to the small, custom-made laptop.

Tim stopped when he saw, on one of the drone's many chips, the words 'Whitelock Industries'. He read it aloud.

'Yeah, Bernard Whitelock?' Dee looked up, clicking the laptop. 'What's the problem?'

'He ... he was part of Clarice's plan – she married him, he built the teleporter. He helped make the imagination box too. Your granddad knew him well.'

'Seriously?' Dee said. 'Well, not any more. He's a megafamous inventor now – top bloke. He's the reason we have AI drones like this, and cloning, electric cars, fusion power – you know, clean, free energy and all that stuff. People say he saved the world. He's a big deal.'

'He didn't used to be,' Tim said. 'Clarice basically kept him prisoner. Are they married?'

'Not as far as I know.'

'Huh, Clarice must have actually loved him – at least enough to make him a success,' Tim said.

'But not enough to stay married to him?' Dee asked.

'I guess she works in mysterious ways.'

They left the broken police drone there in that field and ran back to the Dawn Star Hotel. Inside room ninety-eight they investigated the downloaded plans – they had the complete layout of Crowfield Tower in an interactive document. On the fifty-fifth floor there was something marked as 'The Vault'.

'Clever,' Dee said. 'Top floor could be accessed from the roof, basement could be accessed from the ground floor. Hide the imagination station right in the heart of the building. Makes sense.'

'Now,' Tim said, 'the hard bit.'

Chapter 12

Tim, Dee, Eisenstone and Phil left room ninety-eight – now known as 'base camp'. After a couple of attempts, Tim managed to create a key so they could take a car from the Dawn Star Hotel's car park. This was stealing – there were no two ways about it – but Tim used the word 'commandeered' which sounded somehow less wrong. Plus, they targeted an expensive-looking one, reasoning that a rich person could afford such a loss.

'Also, comfortable,' Dee said, stroking the seat.

Each time Tim did something illegal he inwardly blamed Clarice – she had forced him into this position. Still, he felt a little niggle with every crime. He really hoped karma wasn't real. Or, if it was, somehow it could take into account all the background reasons for his wrongdoing.

After they'd inspected the floor plans for Crowfield Tower, Tim had used the imagination box prototype to create his *own* imagination box. Like his last version had always been, this device was stowed away in his rucksack. And, again like the last model, the reader was a straightforward black beanie. A remotely operated, sleek, strong and portable imagination box – just what they needed for the outlandish burglary they had planned. The only real flaw he could see was that it was slightly warped in shape. Otherwise it was perfect – he had really concentrated on it, after all.

Of course, Dee and Eisenstone were completely astonished. In fact, when the professor saw the new one working he almost fainted. But, having done exactly this once before, Tim shrugged it off and said, 'Come on, it's obvious. Wishing for more wishes? It's gonna happen eventually.'

Eisenstone drove them up to London, where some of the sights and tourist spots were familiar, but others slightly different, slightly wrong. And, without exhaust fumes polluting the air, everywhere seemed to be much cleaner. One thing stuck out: Trafalgar Square's famous bronze lion statues were now crows – just as big, just as proud, just as black.

They arrived at their destination but couldn't find anywhere to park. Eventually, Tim suggested they just leave it on double yellow lines.

'Yeah.' Dee shrugged. 'Who cares, it's not our car.' She found breaking the rules far easier than Tim did.

'But, but the poor owner will and they'll get a ticket,' the professor said.

They were being quite reckless about all this – they had, over the course of the last days, meticulously outlined how they were going to break *into* Crowfield Tower, but they had absolutely no escape planned.

'We won't need a route *out*,' Tim had explained. 'Once we're inside, we'll find the imagination station and use it to return everything to how it was.'

'Besides, there's *no way* we'll be able to escape anyway,' Dee added. 'Not with all the security and alarms that'll be going off.'

'Precisely,' Tim said. 'This trip is one-way.'

The professor seemed uncomfortable with it all, but stayed silent.

So, parking the car on double yellow lines would be – like all these crimes – completely irrelevant when everything was reset back to normal with the imagination station. Eisenstone pulled up the handbrake and checked his face in the mirror.

This evening had been chosen specifically. Tonight there was a charity fundraising event, an auction – to be attended by none other than Clarice Crowfield – in the Green Hall Gallery. This huge building sat right next to Crowfield Tower and was connected to it by a vast garden, like a park, enclosed in glass. It looked like a massive greenhouse – the transparent roof was twenty or so storeys high, with tall, exotic plants growing below. Crucially for their purposes, there was a crane conducting works on it which they could use to break into Crowfield Tower.

So their plan was:

Go to the dinner in the Green Hall Gallery. Sneak off and head upstairs to the roof. Then climb up and along the arm of the crane to a window on about the thirtieth floor of Crowfield Tower, and smash their way inside. Once there they could run upstairs to the fifty-fifth floor, break into the vault, use the imagination station and be back in the old universe in, as Phil said, 'two shakes of a dingo's bingo' – whatever that meant. What could possibly go wrong?

'Loads of things,' Dee had said.

Obviously though, as they were wanted for murder, they needed disguises. This is why Eisenstone was wearing a shaggy brown wig, a fake beard and thick black glasses – as well as a smart tuxedo for the dinner event. Of course he looked ridiculous, but the new hair and its colour did give him a certain youth which Tim reckoned the professor quite liked.

Dee and Tim also had suitable disguises. They were both dressed in smart clothes – Tim in a chequered maroon shirt, grey waistcoat and black trousers. Dee was in a polka-dotted gown, which she had explicitly demanded – but she was also wearing short jeans and a top beneath, which could be changed into for 'increased manoeuvrability'. As for their faces, a little make-up, putty and latex can go a long way when you've got an imagination box to hand. The glue on Tim's fake nose pulled on his skin and he could see the stuck-on eyebrows if he glanced up, but besides all that they looked great.

And, even though it was completely unnecessary as he would be in the top pocket of Tim's waistcoat the whole time, Phil was wearing a miniature tuxedo and a trilby hat.

'I wish my appearance to be that of a medium-ranking Italian-American gangster,' the monkey had said. 'Albeit a small one.'

From the car Tim could see people queuing to get inside the gallery at the end of the road. There was a red carpet and velvet ropes lining the pavement. Beyond, a huge historic building glowed orange thanks to up-pointing lamps on the front. And to the left of that – connected by the glass atrium – was Crowfield Tower. It seemed to disappear into the night sky – odd lights on the top floor could well be mistaken for stars. About a quarter of the way up, running right to left like a bridge, was the crane.

The tower's entrance was fenced off with a gate, tyre spikes and a few armed Grey Guards. Tim also counted three police drones circling the building itself – luckily they seemed to be staying low.

'Good job we're not going in the front door,' Tim said, shaking his head at all that security. Not for the first time, he felt suddenly unsure about what they were doing, about how utterly insane they would seem if they were captured. It'd be embarrassing as much as anything else.

'So, we've got everything all lined up,' Dee said, looking at Crowfield Tower's floor plan on her mobile phone. 'Except for one thing: the vault door. It's about a foot thick and, I assume, made of metal.'

Tim nodded. 'Yeah. That's why I created this.' He pulled a block of plastic explosives from his rucksack – it was wrapped in cling film. It looked just like a big lump of mustard-coloured plasticine.

'What the hell is that?' Dee asked.

'Semtex,' Tim said, wiggling it. 'Or my version of it at least. Timtex.'

'Like, a bomb?' Dee's eyes were wide.

'Yeah. How did you think we were going to get through the vault door?'

'Oh, delightful,' Phil said, tilting his hat back with his thumb. 'High time we had some explosions.'

'It's … I don't know,' Dee said. 'Taking explosives in a rucksack to a charity dinner – it just *sounds* bad. It sounds like *we're* the baddies.'

'Well, of course, if you say it like that, it does,' Tim admitted.

Eisenstone was shaking his head. 'I really … I really think it best if you don't imagine bombs with the machine,' he said. 'How do you know it's stable? Indeed, what if it goes off in your hand?'

'Relax. I haven't even *made* a detonator yet. It's completely safe.' Tim banged it a few times on the inside of the car door, to show how confident he was.

'Stop it,' Dee said, snatching it from him. She shoved it back in his rucksack. 'You haven't exactly got a perfect track record with your creations.'

As before, Tim noticed Eisenstone's slightly glazed, distant expression. The professor seemed lost in his own thoughts, even at a time like this.

It was a black-tie event. The gallery was full of fine-dining tables, all laid out with expensive cutlery and arrangements, crystal glasses and thick cloth napkins. It looked more like a glitzy award ceremony. Using fake invites and confusing the metal detectors with an EMP disrupter Tim had invented and created, they successfully entered and were seated at the back of the room. Dee whispered that it was a good job they *weren't* wrong'uns, as it had been quite easy to smuggle the bomb and the new imagination box into this place.

Before they could leap into action, the lights dimmed and ambient, orchestral music came from speakers near the stage.

Tim turned in his chair to see the doors at the side of the grand hall open and Clarice Crowfield swoop in – people stood and applauded. Not wanting to draw attention to themselves, Tim, Dee and Eisenstone did so too.

Just the sight of her sent Tim's heart rate up – he was sweating, hardly breathing now. He was so afraid that he couldn't clap his limp hands, so he just cupped them at his chest and watched on. Clarice looked just like the portrait painting he'd once seen of her – her long, straight black hair hanging down, her sharp cheekbones and her proud, surveying gaze. Her dark laced dress was almost Gothic in style, slightly weird like everyone else's clothes, with a high collar and squared shoulders.

The one main difference was that she appeared, well, *nice* for want of a better word. Kind. Tim couldn't really explain what it was, but she seemed to have warmth in her eyes and her wrinkles looked as though they were from years of smiling, not years of snarling. It was incredibly unsettling and completely the opposite of what he had expected to see, much like the impossible horror of Elisa not recognising him. Like so much in this universe, it was just wrong.

'Welcome, ladies and gentlemen, to the annual Crowfield Foundation Fundraiser,' Clarice said at the lectern on stage. 'Please, as always, give generously as this year we are raising money for disadvantaged children living in poverty around the world.'

'You're right,' Dee whispered to Tim, with a slight smile. 'We have to stop this monster.'

He had to admit, Clarice *was* different. But he didn't let all the questions he had cloud his judgement – they still had to go ahead with the plan.

Later in the evening there was a guided tour of the gallery itself, which seemed a great opportunity to sneak off. They left the crowd in the portrait hall, where they were being shown various head and shoulder paintings of historic figures. Tim wondered which were real and which imagined. And, of course, there was an entire wing dedicated to portraits of Clarice – this was a feature of her fantasy that seemed to fit perfectly.

They rounded a corner – the stairwell was just up ahead. Tim and Dee were chatting as they strode along the polished, chequered marble floor.

'Everyone *does* seem to love her,' he said.

'I guess this is maybe how she perceives herself?' Dee wondered. 'In my fantasies I am a little bit taller, my hair is a little bit cooler. You said Clarice always wanted power, wanted to be a popular politician – her dream has come true.'

'I dunno. When the Clarice I remember used

her giant imagination box, she accidently created a demonic creature and it destroyed her house and tried to kill her.'

'This shines some light on her self-esteem,' Phil added.

'Anyway, the imagination station – what does it look like?' Dee asked. 'What exactly are we searching for?'

'Not sure really,' Tim said.

'What?' She grabbed his arm and slowed to a stop.

'Well, I've never actually *seen* it,' Tim said. 'Only a drawing. But I suspect it'll probably have a square bit with all the computer stuff in it, then another glassy bit on top which, I guess, will have a brain inside – a copy of my brain, to be precise. Then a reader. Also, I'm fairly sure I saw a wire, so it needs to be plugged in? Charged up maybe?'

Tim checked behind to see Eisenstone staring idly at a huge landscape painting.

'Sir,' a voice from beyond said. Tim and Dee side-stepped behind the corner arch, peering round. A suited security guard emerged and told the professor he shouldn't be wandering about, as the gallery was technically closed.

'Oh no,' Tim whispered.

Eisenstone flicked an eye their way and gave them a quick nod as he was escorted back down the hallway. They were on their own now.

Tim, Dee and Phil made it all the way up the gallery's floors, through various exhibits and art from different eras. Although they were moving quickly, one or two works caught their attention. There was a sculpture of a chess set but, instead of normal pieces, every square on the board was occupied by a hazy grey hologram – sixty-four little flickering cuboids.

'I don't get it,' Tim said.

'I think ...' Dee whispered, passing her fingers through the ghostly light, 'I think it's like a game of chess, but all the pieces are in every possible place all at the same time.'

'Infinity Chess,' Phil read from the plaque. 'Chinfinity. Ha.'

'Come on,' Dee said.

They arrived on the roof, where thankfully it

was quiet besides a slight breeze and a distant siren somewhere below. And, as they had previously established, a large yellow crane formed a sort of balance beam from this roof to the sheer face of Crowfield Tower.

They pulled their disguises off their faces and Dee shook her real hair out of the wig.

'Right, well, I guess we've got to climb,' she said, rolling her gown down and stepping out of it – she was wearing jeans and a blue T-shirt now.

There had been talk of jetpacks, zip wires and more. But all these ideas, as well as being dangerous, would draw a lot of attention.

So Tim put his reader hat on and then gripped the cold ladder – his feet clanged as he climbed and climbed. Along the way, he stopped to catch his breath and saw 'Whitelock Industries – Automated Construction' stamped on the yellow metal by his hand. Looking up the ladder, he noticed there was no place for an operator. This crane must be robotic. Luckily it seemed to be switched off.

'Come on,' Dee said from below.

He carried on pulling himself up and up until, eventually, he arrived at the top, on the horizontal platform of the crane, panting and sighing. Dee clambered up just behind him – he helped her to her feet. The whole thing creaked and swayed, rattled and shuddered in the exposed weather. They shuffled around the main section, holding on to the rails.

Then they climbed up a shorter ladder and on to the base of the crane's long arm. Clearly, *this* section was not designed for people – there was no walkway, no safety barriers. Tim looked along the lattice of metalwork, all the way across to Crowfield Tower.

Here we go, he thought. He went first, stepping carefully along the crane arm, shuffling round each vertical piece of metal, holding on tight and taking it slow.

'Don't look down,' Dee yelled.

Wind howled and whistled through the struts as they went.

'Oh God, oh *God, no*,' Tim shouted.

'What? What is it?'

'I just looked down.'

'I said *don't* loo—kuuurrrh. I just did it too. We're so high up.'

'What is all the fuss abo— GOODNESS GRACIOUS,' Phil added.

'Calm, keep calm,' Dee said. 'Always have three limbs in contact at all times. And don't rush.'

Gusts strong enough to remind Tim of the seaside flapped his clothes and pushed against his back. But still, they went on. About three quarters of the way along, Tim began to notice white splodges on the thick steel beneath his shoes. By this point, the crane was hanging over the transparent roof of the indoor gardens below. It was a deadly fall just to get to the glass, and then *another* deadly drop should you go through it, which, from this height, you probably would.

'Right, we're nearly there,' Tim said, placing his foot on to what he'd now decided was spatters of paint. But why would there be paint up here, he wondered.

On that thought, something cooed above his head. He looked up as a pigeon erupted, flapping close enough for him to feel feathers on his face. Flinching away, he yelped and then – at precisely the moment he realised it was bird droppings he was standing on – slipped.

'Tim!' Dee yelled.

He clanged to a sitting position, his arms flailing as he tilted off the crane. It all happened in a blink, with a surge of instant panic – like when you lean too far back on your chair. In a hopeless moment, he knew that it was happening *and* that he couldn't stop it.

His face scrunched in terror and he groaned, unsure which way was up. But, when he looked, he *wasn't* falling.

Instead, somehow, his rucksack had snagged on a protruding bolt and saved him. Dangling there, like a parachutist, he had nothing to grab, nowhere to put his feet. His legs kicked desperately in thin air as his armpits began to ache from the straps, which were supporting his whole weight.

Whimpering, Tim wiped disgusting pigeon gunk off his hands and tried to look round to Dee. But, with his shifting weight, there was a loud rip from above and, one by one, the rucksack's straps snapped. He fell lower, grabbing a tattered strap just in time.

Now Tim was holding on by just his fingers, dangling at least fifty feet above a flat glass roof, and a further two hundred feet below that was concrete and distant plant life.

'Stupid pigeon idiot!' Tim yelled.

Anger was little use. He was slipping.

Phil had ended up on his shoulder and was scrabbling around for ways to help.

'Wait there,' Dee said. She was stepping along the crane towards him.

'Hurry,' Tim shouted, his heart punching his throat, his fingers sliding, aching. 'Gah, I'm slipping, I'm slipping, I'm slipping.'

'Timothy, create something!' Phil yelled, clinging on to his collar.

But the second Tim closed his eyes to imagine, there was another, longer ripping sound and the imagination box slid out of a frayed hole in the side of the bag. The cube went down fast, spinning and glistening below him. It hit the flat glass directly beneath, with a tiny, almost silent thud.

Dee was his final hope. She had almost reached him. The last thing Tim saw was her desperate hand stretching out for his. But, with a final rip of stitching, the bag was torn in two, and he fell.

Chapter 13

What struck Tim, who was of course falling to his death, was how peaceful these final moments were. Strange, really, to think that after all he'd been through, after all he'd survived, it was an especially slippery patch of pigeon slop that would ultimately introduce him to his maker. He'd always thought his demise would be somehow more glamorous than this.

The wind, blasting through his hair and clothes, felt as thick as water. Above, Dee was disappearing fast into the night sky. And below, well, he didn't want to think about that, but it was a flat glass roof and it was rushing towards him at quite a speed.

It astonished Tim just how many thoughts he had during that rapid descent – it was as though time slowed down – maybe it was the adrenaline. Or maybe his memory of the incident had changed. After all they say dreams only last a brief moment and yet often seem like hours.

Good job, actually, because it gave him time to have these very important thoughts:

Pigeons suck. Pigeons have feathers. Feathers are in pillows. Pillows are soft.

Lots of pillows.

He landed with a terrible crunch, his knees jutting into his chin and sending him flat. A metallic taste filled his mouth.

For at least a few seconds, he assumed he was dead.

But no. Tim was looking up at a long yellow crane arm – Dee was there, looking back down at him, almost invisible in the dark sky. He assessed the damage. His legs were still attached. He could move his arms. His eyes were fine. This was all good news.

'My hat,' Phil yelled. 'My hat has gone.'

His ears worked too.

Sitting up, Tim noticed he was lying on a very large pile of pillows. At the edge of the squidgy mound was the imagination box, the device's lid snapped – a squished, half-formed pillow still protruding from the opening. Hundreds of them must have materialised so quickly that they forced their way out, creating a sort of crash mat. While far from ideal, it had saved his life – he patted them in appreciation.

'I cannot see it anywhere.' The monkey was darting around, growing quite panicked and grabbing his head.

'Phil,' Tim groaned.

'Oh, Timothy, you survived as well? Positive stuff, old chappy bean. But, alas, my hat.'

'Don't worry, I'll make you another.'

'When? Now?'

'Later.'

Brushing himself off, Tim stood. Dee was too far away to shout – plus he didn't want to draw attention to them. The area below was dark, closed to the public luckily. However, if someone on the street with a keen eye were to look up, their plan could be ruined.

So he gave her a thumbs up and then clambered over the pillows towards the imagination box. With every movement, which was cumbersome on this squishy terrain, he heard what sounded like creaking ice. It wasn't until he noticed a thousand hairline cracks running outwards beneath him that he realised he was still in a fair bit of trouble.

He retrieved the device extremely carefully, and hid it away in a replacement rucksack – along with the Timtex he'd made earlier to blast through the vault door. Considering how weak that last rucksack proved to be (another poorly created item), Tim was impressed that his imagination box had survived the fall. Its *new* bag was made of bulletproof, fireproof, tearproof material. He flung it on to his back and tightened the straps.

Then he stepped slowly off the island of pillows. As gently as possible, he lowered his toes towards the glass. Below, two hundred feet below in fact, was the hard ground. Why make a roof out of glass, Tim wondered.

As his shoe made contact, one, two, three tiny cracks appeared, running across the expanse like crevices in an earthquake.

His stomach felt hollow and his chest tight.

'This is not a good situation,' Phil said on Tim's shoulder.

'That was a helpful comment, thank you. As long as I tread slowly and distribute—' A terrible crack from below froze him. 'As long as I distribute my weight,' Tim whispered, 'we should be fine.'

'Why are you whispering?'

'I dunno. I feel better if I whisper.'

'OK,' Phil whispered. 'Timothy?'

'What?'

'You know the new hat you promised to make for me?'

'Later.'

'It is just that if we are about to die I worry that—'

'Phil!'

'Of course, continue.'

A few more paces and Tim decided to crawl on all fours, watching lines appear beneath each hand and knee. Eventually, he managed to make it on to the next pane, which only had a few cracks. The one after that had none and then he was able to get to his feet and run the remainder of the way, leaving the sizable amount of pillows and damage behind him.

Now safe-ish, he created a grappling-hook gun and, valiantly, pointed it upwards declaring, 'Hold on, Phil.'

Once the hook and spiralling rope had disappeared above him, snaking round the crane arm, he pressed the trigger. However, Tim didn't realise just how strong you have to be for this kind of thing. Instead of dragging him heroically into the air, it was just snatched from his hand and flung off somewhere into the night sky.

'Pfft,' Tim said, rolling his shoulder and wincing. 'Batman is a pack of lies.'

'Basic physics, Timothy,' Phil said.

Luckily the second try saw Tim create a mechanical winch that he clipped in place around his belt and, with a flick of a switch, he was lifted straight up. It wasn't the fastest mechanism, but it got them up there in one piece, where they were reunited with Dee near the tall face of Crowfield Tower.

'Be more careful,' Dee said. Which was good advice. Together they approached the windows, which were actually a metre or so away from the end of the crane's arm. They glanced up the daunting height of the building.

'Right,' Tim said, pulling a sharp hammer from his rucksack. 'I'll throw this at the window – then we'll jump inside.'

'Got it,' Dee said.

'The alarm will probably go off immediately, so once it's happened, we *run*.'

Leaning back and lifting a leg like a baseball bowler, Tim threw the hammer with all his strength. However, as though he'd thrown it at a trampoline, it bounced straight back and clanged, spinning off the crane near their heads. They both flinched and ducked.

'Pretty hard glass that,' Dee said.

'All right, how about *this*?' Tim closed his eyes, imagined, and then pulled a gun-like device from his imagination box.

'What is it?' Dee was frowning.

'Not entirely sure,' Tim admitted, feeling its weight in both hands. 'I imagined a glass blaster, whatever that is.'

Turning his head and bracing himself, he took aim and squeezed the trigger. The bang jarred his arm, the window shattered and, as predicted, a very loud alarm blared out.

'Go, go, go!'

Pushing off the crane, they leapt the gap, landing on a lower carpeted hallway inside an office. Glass shards crunched underfoot as they bolted for the stairs.

Both Tim and Dee were barely jogging by the time they reached the right floor, panting and tugging themselves up the banister. But they made it, shouldering through a door and turning a corner and spotting a huge silver circle at the end of the corridor.

'That's it, that's the vault door,' Dee said, checking the location on the floor plan she had on her mobile.

Tim placed the rucksack on the ground, removed the plastic explosives, then ran and stuck it on the thick slab of metal. It reminded him of a giant safe – like something from a bank. When he returned, he closed his eyes and imagined a detonator, then dragged Dee behind the wall.

Tim held up the little stick and hovered his thumb over the red button on top. For a moment he wondered just how powerful the bomb would be. Of course it was a difficult thing to judge – he thought maybe they should get a little bit further away to ensure they were safe from any—

'A little less conversation, a little more action please,' Dee said as she slapped the detonator's button.

The explosion was incredible. Debris and rubble and the loudest bang Tim'd ever heard blasted down the corridor at their side – he shielded his face and leant away. Smoke came rushing past a second later, in a dark rumbling gust.

'Wonderful,' Phil said with a cough.

When they stepped round to look, the vault door was hanging open, strip lights above were dangling from wires, the carpet was gone, bricks and concrete were strewn along the floor. A few small fires were also crackling away, peppered among blackened smears and glowing in the brownish dust. It smelled like barbecues and building sites.

'Quick style,' Dee said.

A slight fizz in Tim's chest and a ringing in his ears continued as he covered his mouth with a sleeve and ran into the vault. The previous alarm was joined now by a fire bell and, a second later, sprinklers burst on above them.

Inside there were rows and rows of shelves, some of which had been knocked over. It seemed mostly to be paperwork, boring boxes of useless junk. Tim and Dee went off searching, scanning the vault for the imagination station. Before long, Tim was soaked to his skin, shivering in the spraying water. It ran down his face, in his mouth, in his eyes. He could taste his own sweat and the dampened smoke.

He started to breathe fast, almost whimpering, when he couldn't see anything that looked even remotely like the device. Where is it? *Where is it?* he repeated in his head.

All the containers were too small. Most of the shelves held only folders. There was nowhere it could be.

It was just simply, 'Not here,' Tim whispered, staring at the wall.

'What?' Dee yelled from the other side of the vault.

'It's … it's not here.'

'So …' Dee stepped back towards him. 'What does that mean?'

'It could mean a lot of things, none of them good.'

'We didn't plan for this,' Dee was shouting over the alarms and artificial rain. 'The guards will be on their way … the police. Tim, what we've just done is enough to go to prison. Like, kid's prison. Young offenders or whatever. Even *if* we convinced them we had no part in Fredric's murder, we have still done all this.' She gestured at the mess.

'We need—'

'This is why most people *don't* do crimes,' Dee continued, talking to herself now. 'Not because it's necessarily difficult, but because the consequences suck so much. We are in an *enormous* amount of trouble. That can't be stressed enough.'

Her cold, straight summary made Tim feel sick. Up until this moment he'd taken comfort in the vague idea that *none of this* was real. But it was. It was *too real*.

'OK, OK,' he yelled. 'We'll … we'll run, we'll head for the roof and—'

'Watch out!'

Tim turned to see the vault door – a huge slab of thick, chrome-polished steel – tilt and fall towards him. He took a step back, stumbled into a shelf, but was knocked to the ground. He screamed – a sharp squeezing pain clutched his foot.

The door had started a domino effect with the shelf units, two of which had fallen and sandwiched Tim's lower half in place.

'I'm stuck,' he said, sitting up and tugging. 'My leg! It's completely trapped.'

'Right.' Dee took the rucksack off his back. 'We're just going to have to chop it off. Quickly, create an axe.'

'An axe? What? We're not cutting my leg off, Dee. And surely, if anything, we should at least *attempt* to break these shelves.'

'*Of course* we'd try that first,' Dee huffed. 'I'm just saying, don't hold your breath on that leg.'

'No.'

'Timothy,' Phil said, 'you do have another one.'

'No! I'll create a drill, and you can dismantle these shelves and free me that way. It'll take a bit longer but—'

Dee sighed in defeat, slumping on her knees. Her hair was slick wet now, her clothes shining and clinging to her goosebumped flesh. 'Never mind,' she said. 'Look.'

Arching his neck, Tim saw that in the open doorway of the vault stood maybe five or six armed officers – Grey Guards – all wearing gas masks and heavy vests. They paused there, guns pointed low, clearly in disbelief at the destruction and the two children – and a tuxedo-clad finger monkey – sitting amid it all.

'Um,' Tim said, propped up on his elbows. 'Sorry?'

Chapter 14

Sorry, apparently, didn't quite cut it. However, the Grey Guards were relatively kind to them. Perhaps they were relieved that Tim and Dee didn't seem to pose much of a threat. Maybe they had expected someone far more dangerous would be behind such a break-in. Nevertheless, they still arrested them.

'We're bringing them down,' one of the guards said into his radio after they'd all heaved Tim out from under the rubble in Crowfield Tower's vault.

'No, no,' a voice crackled back. 'Take them to the helipad – the street is crawling with press now. Let's keep them off the ten o'clock news.'

As they were escorted out of the vault and through some offices, Tim's shoes squished in puddles on the soaked carpet – the sprinklers had pretty much destroyed everything the bomb had missed. Honestly, he did feel a little bit guilty. Near the lift, he had a chance to peer out through the window. Below, he could see the crane, the pile of pillows on the lower glass roof and, sure enough, all kinds of commotion on the street. Blue siren lights flickered and reflected off everything – there were perhaps twenty police cars, two fire engines and countless police officers. As well as this, there were hundreds of civilians, camera crews, photographers, all the guests from the neighbouring charity do they'd attended – they really had caused quite a scene.

Tim was still wet and, as he began to sweat, it seemed he might never dry. This really was serious stuff, he thought, feeling a confusing mix of emotions – mostly though he felt sorry. Not just for all the damage, but for failing so spectacularly.

'They evacuated every building in this street,' the guard said – only one of them seemed to speak. 'What the *hell* were you kids thinking? Where did you get a bomb?'

'It's a long story.' Tim sighed, as they stepped into the elevator. 'One you almost certainly wouldn't believe.'

He glanced up at the man – Tim had forgotten that all these guards were clones. They were all wearing helmets with visors which hid their faces, and Tim wondered if they all looked identical too. It must get confusing, he thought. Maybe they've got numbers? He looked then at the guard's uniform – sure enough, on his arm there was a badge. It had a grey 'GG' in the middle, a small crow, then a four-digit number beneath.

'Try me,' the guard, Mr 2767, added, pressing the button for the top floor.

Tim shrugged, then told him everything. Front to back. The whole story. And why not? They couldn't possibly get in any *more* trouble.

'You're right,' the man said. 'I don't believe you. Come on.'

On the roof of Crowfield Tower, Tim and Dee were bundled into the back of a helicopter. It hissed and beeped as it warmed up, then the blades roared and rumbled above them. The pilot said his name was Barry, then slammed the sliding door, locking them in. He had the imagination box and climbed into the cockpit with one of the Grey Guards.

This evening really had gone wrong, Tim thought to himself, staring out of the window. He wondered where on earth the imagination station might be – then he sighed at how much weight they'd given to the map he'd created with the imagination box. How flawed and sloppy his mind had become. For all his efforts, for all the rules and laws they'd broken, they'd essentially achieved nothing.

Actually, no, it was worse than that, Tim thought. They'd made their predicament even more difficult to escape. Dee was right, they'd just bombed a government building. Even *if* you explained the reasons, Tim realised how bad that sounded. He could quite clearly picture a judge – wig, gown, everything – reading out a list of what they'd done. People in court would gasp and shake their heads. 'Yeah, *but* ...' Tim might try and say, looking up with his best 'sorry' face. It'd be no use.

With a slight tilt and sway, the helicopter lifted and flew off across the London skyline. Tim looked down at all the lights, the weaving river, black and glinting in the night. The image was not that different to the map he'd made. Maybe it was just a premonition, maybe this was always how it would end.

Sitting opposite, Dee was also thinking silently to herself – picking at her sleeve, planning something maybe. However, Phil had found his way into the cockpit and was in the middle of a long conversation with Barry – oddly they seemed to get on well. (Once Barry had come to terms with a talking finger monkey, of course, which always takes a bit of time).

'Yes, precisely,' Phil was saying. 'Little black rim, white band round the bowl – just like a gangster hat.'

'Tim, what are we going to do?' Dee whispered. 'Do you honestly think Clarice will kill us?'

'I'd assume so, wouldn't you?' Tim said. 'She snuffed Fredric on a whim. She can't have us telling everyone the truth.'

'We could just ask them what'll happen to us?' Dee suggested. 'Then we can react accordingly.'

'No harm in trying.'

'Excuse me,' Dee leant forwards in her seat, peering into the cockpit. 'Where are we going?'

'Taking you to GGHQ,' Barry said, pressing a couple of buttons. 'You just sit tight.'

'What will they do with us?'

'Who knows?' The pilot turned in his seat. He was wearing a black helmet with a strange, high-tech visor. 'I ain't got a clue what's going on. All I know is that there are four levels of security clearance. And you guys are marked as a level *five*. Someone wants you bad. I don't get paid enough to know why.'

'What about me?' Phil asked. The monkey was sitting in amongst all the dials and buttons in the helicopter's cockpit.

'Oh, there's no mention of you, furry man,' Barry said. 'You're in the clear.'

'Superb.' Phil smiled. 'I should go on record, however, as expressing an explicit desire to stay close to young Timothy and Dee.'

'All right, let's assume the worst,' Dee whispered, shuffling back next to Tim. 'We can*not* allow them to take us to HQ, wherever that is. That can't happen.'

'Shall we open the door and jump out?' Tim said. 'Might land in water?'

Dee put her face against the glass, and looked down at the city below. 'Yeah but, like, we might not?'

Tim could still hear Phil chatting with Barry and the guard. 'Might I enquire: what type of helicopter is this?' the monkey asked.

'This is a Cobra 2000,' Barry said, proudly. 'Whitelock Industries' finest.'

'A Cobra – what an interesting name.' Phil stroked his chin. 'I would have called it a spinny float box.'

'Ha, nice,' Barry said. 'Or ... or a shouty hover van?'

'Oh jolly, yes, wonderful work.'

'Seriously though, I think it's called a Cobra to sound cool,' Barry said.

Still wearing his reader hat, Tim noticed that the imagination box was in between the two seats in the cockpit.

'Come on,' Dee said. 'Think. *Think.*'

'All right, I've got a plan. We ...' Tim began but

stopped when, out of the corner of his eye, he saw something terrible.

'What? What is it?' Dee asked.

In the cockpit, emerging from the imagination box as though being charmed from a basket, a cobra was standing tall. An *actual* cobra. The snake came up to the same height as Barry and the guard's heads. Between the men, it looked left, then right, swaying slightly in that predatory way cobras do. Its pale-scaled skin was shining with all the colours of the helicopter's controls. So far, no one besides Tim and Dee had noticed the creature.

'Tim,' Dee said through clenched teeth. 'That does not appear to be a solution.'

'I know, but they just kept saying "cobra" and I kept picturing one and, well, you can see what's happened.'

'Guys,' Dee said quietly, leaning forwards, trying to sound reassuring. 'You need to keep calm, and, most importantly of all, don't make any sudden—'

'OH, NOW WHAT IS THAT?!'

The helicopter lurched violently to the left, Tim and Dee slammed against the opposite window – then it flung them suddenly back to the other side, like ragdolls. In the cockpit, the cobra had struck twice, biting Barry on the arm and shoulder. Clearly terrified, he had abandoned the controls and was pressed against the door.

'Relax,' Tim yelled. 'It's not poisonous.'

'How do you know?' Dee shouted back – she was upside down, getting rocked and thrashed about on the floor. Her shoe flung off into the air.

They were in a crazed spin; Tim watched the horizon zip round, tilting and wobbling – sky, earth, moon, sky, earth, moon. All he could be sure of was that they were falling. That was obvious as he and Dee were pressed against the ceiling now. Up front, there was still just unmitigated cobra carnage in the cockpit. The snake was out of its box and it was going absolutely mental, striking wildly in all directions. Warning lights and beeps were sounding as they fell.

The ground was sickeningly close when their spin evened out. A frantic drumming came around them, and then leaves and twigs and broken branches were bouncing off the windscreen. Beeping, shouting, beeping, shouting. Then, with a final crunch, they were completely stationary. The rotor blades were still spinning loudly, but they appeared to have crash-landed quite neatly in a tree.

Barry opened his window and threw the cobra outside, shuddering as he did so. Phil darted back towards Tim, slipping straight into his top pocket.

Dazed and perhaps in shock, Dee slid open the door and started to clamber out, even though they were still high up.

'Where are you going?' Tim asked, quickly following her on to a slightly lower branch.

However, with a quick creak the wood gave way and they both fell through twigs and landed in a heap on some grass.

Tim looked around – they were in a park. There didn't seem to be anyone in sight. It was late after all. The helicopter – still very much running – was right above. But, with another snapping branch, it tilted and came falling down the face of the tree. Deadly spinning blades, like an upturned blender, roared towards Tim and Dee as they scrambled to their feet. Behind, Tim watched the chopper come down heavily, the rotor tearing a trench into the ground, mud and turf thrown up like water from a sprinkler. The blades spiralled off and the helicopter rolled over entirely, the main rotor just buckled stumps. It whirred to silence amid a huge amount of mess and smoky steam.

'Wow,' Dee said, picking a leaf out of her hair. 'That actually went quite well, all things considered.'

After checking that Barry and the guard were OK, Tim reached in and grabbed the imagination box. Perched on top of the broken husk of steel, he created some anti-venom and passed it back inside. The two men were visibly shaken, but alive. It was clear they were both trapped in the half-crushed cockpit.

'I just want you to know that I am very sorry about that,' Tim said.

'Help us out of here,' the guard yelled.

'Yeah, come on, guys,' Barry added.

Dee appeared at the windscreen, which was pressed sideways into the earth. 'No, sorry,' she said. 'As long as you're both OK, then we're going to leave you here and run away.' She jutted a thumb over her shoulder. 'Little runsies – escape sort of thing, yeah?'

'Oh, please don't,' Barry said, struggling with his seat belt. 'I'll get fired.'

'Nah,' Tim said. 'This isn't your fault. The cobra was my bad. Just explain what happened and they'll understand.'

'Toodles, gentlemen,' Phil added. 'Send Pam my regards.'

Mouthing 'sorry' one final time, Tim slid off the helicopter and pulled the straps on his rucksack tight.

'Wait, come back,' a muffled voice yelled. But they were already running.

Chapter 15

Two very strange things happened as they travelled back to the Dawn Star Hotel. On the way, they rushed straight into a public toilet where Tim created a change of clothes, as well as hats and glasses to conceal their identity. Also – and by now he was way past feeling guilty about such things – Tim made a few big wads of cash to buy train tickets to Glassbridge. Again, he shook his head at Clarice's face on the notes.

After this they headed towards the train station, passing through a familiar part of London. It was so familiar, in fact, that Tim had to stop and study his surroundings. It took a few seconds, but then he realised they were standing on a quiet side street right next to where the Diamond Building *should* be. But TRAD's headquarters were now nothing more than a block of flats. The area looked rough – broken windows and boarded-up, derelict shops, covered in graffiti and dirt. Up ahead, Dee turned and waited near a doorway which was glowing red with a flickering neon light. Tim was about to explain why he'd stopped, but—

'Spare any change, lad?' a husky voice whispered from low down. Tim was startled. He hadn't even realised a person was there, sitting on the damp pavement next to a scraggy dog.

The tramp was huddled over, wearing a thick brown jacket and holding a small cup in his lap, which was covered by an old blue sleeping bag. Like his skinny dog, he had scruffy hair on his head and his face. His fingers were black with grime and shivering, even though it wasn't cold.

'Um ... I,' Tim started. But then he paused and squinted in the faintly red light. '*Rick?* God, Rick, is that you?'

The man was alarmed by this, and nodded warily.

'Aye, do I know you?' he said, his accent just how it used to be.

Tim snatched his disguise glasses off, exposing his face, but then sighed when there was no reaction. 'No. You don't,' he whispered. 'Of course you don't.'

Earlier, Tim had blamed Rick Harris for everything. But seeing him like this – this new version of the man – he only felt sorry for him. He looked up at Tim – his eyes were bloodshot and wet with absolute, pure sadness. A sudden guilt hit Tim and all he wanted was to help however he could.

'Come on,' Dee said from further up the street, waving him along.

But, before he left, Tim took his rucksack off his back, crouched and reached inside. He grabbed the big wads of cash – he had no idea exactly how much – and placed them gently into Rick's dirty hands. His mouth hung open. He was so surprised that he looked almost scared. Maybe scared to believe it was actually happening.

'I am sorry,' Tim said. 'Things will get better. I promise.'

Everyone will have a safe place to sleep in the next universe, Tim decided.

'Sorry?' Rick hugged the money against his stomach, still stunned. 'Why are you *sorry*? You're some kind of angel.'

Was this another one of Clarice's punishments, Tim wondered, or had Rick's life just gone differently in this universe? Either way, Tim knew there was more to him than met the eye. He knew there was a reason, a story, a cause for him sitting on the damp pavement.

Tim tried to smile, then stood and caught up with Dee – it was clear Rick wanted to thank him more, but they didn't have the time.

'Who was that?' she asked.

'Nobody,' he whispered. For some reason he didn't feel like discussing this difference.

At the end of the street, they took cover in a dark doorway as a procession of Grey Guards, marching like soldiers, and a huge armoured van, trundled past. Like all the vehicles, it was electric, but so big that it still managed to be loud. Heavy metal tank-tracks rumbled over the tarmac, tingling in Tim's chest and feet. He saw the 'GG' logo stamped on the side. Above, three drones flew, spinning slowly as they went, scanning and searching with slow rhythmic beeps. They'd know by now that the helicopter had crashed.

Tim, Dee and Phil made it to the station and boarded their train to Glassbridge, sitting quickly and not speaking at all. The whole way, which was quite a journey, Tim was poised to spring into action, ready to take flight again and run and hide, things which were becoming quite a habit. At one point two Grey Guards, armed with black machine guns, passed through the train carriage – Tim heard their beeping radios, little crackling conversations echoing from within. One of them stopped and looked right at him. Tim stared back, through the helmet's tinted visor and swallowed his terror. He couldn't see the man's eyes, but it was obvious where they were pointed. This was it, Tim thought. But then the guard hesitated and headed off up the carriage.

'Phew,' Tim said, all his muscles relaxing.

'Maybe they didn't recognise us,' Dee whispered.

Having snuck back into the hotel, they both dived to hug Eisenstone up in room ninety-eight – relieved he hadn't been arrested. The professor, still wearing his tuxedo, said he'd been worried sick when he watched the news and heard that two suspects were in custody over a break-in at Crowfield Tower.

'Clarice herself was on Black Feather News. She said it was all under control,' he explained. 'Am, am I right to assume you were unsuccessful in finding the imagination station?'

'Sadly, yes,' Tim said. 'Not there.'

Although they were in an almost completely hopeless situation, Tim was still able to relax in room ninety-eight. It was now his favourite place in any universe. So much comfort and safety. Being back here was like pressing pause on it all. Again, as before, he wished they could stay forever, tucked away in this cosy nest.

'So … a life behind bars, hey?' Eisenstone said. 'Maybe, indeed, the best place for us.'

'What do you mean by that?' Tim asked, alarmed.

'All my work …' The professor seemed lost. He

kept looking at his hands. 'My entire career … I never wanted to be responsible for such things … the potential for wrongdoing. Maybe … maybe we're not ready for this technology.'

'You can't uninvent things,' Tim said.

Eisenstone narrowed his eyes. 'What if we could? What if we could take it all back? What if I'd never invented it? What if we could live in a world without these machines?'

'You once warned me that in the wrong hands it could be catastrophic,' Tim admitted. 'But in the *right* hands …'

'I, I … I just fear there's no way back for us.'

'There is,' Tim said. 'Honestly. We just need that imagination station and I can create the perfect universe – utopia, paradise. It'll rock.'

'I want to be a movie star,' Dee said. 'Or an astronaut. It's hard – is there any way I can be both?'

'Course,' Tim said. 'Anything is possible. Everyone can get what they want.'

'Tim, no, no.' Eisenstone sighed. 'There's no paradise. There can't be. Don't you see? You may *think* you know what's best for everyone, for the world, but I assure you that you don't. One man's heaven is another man's hell. We must not play God.'

Tim hadn't really thought that much about the universe he would create – what he had planned was to put everything *roughly* back to how it was. Of course, there would need to be slight amendments to keep everyone he loved safe. And then, as well, there would be a few bonuses and tweaks. No harm in making the Dawn Star more successful, giving Elisa a break, and maybe then Chris wouldn't have to work so hard. It had seemed so straightforward. Now the professor had said this, however, it seemed altogether more complicated. What about homeless people, like Rick? What about diseases and earthquakes and war and, and . . . the list went on.

'But we still need to find the device,' Dee said. 'Whatever reality Tim can imagine is *surely* better for *us* than this absolute cluster-mess.'

Tim agreed with that at least.

'If only we could *make* Clarice tell us its location,' Phil added.

Nodding, Tim pointed at the monkey. 'That's it,' he said. 'That's the only way.'

'Somehow I don't think she'll just blurt it out,' Dee said.

'Plus, you cannot simply telephone the Prime Minister can you?' Phil looked to the professor. He shook his head. 'I fear she will have all kinds of security, like the Queen.'

'The Queen?' Dee said.

'Yeah,' Tim added. 'She's got like hundreds of bodyguards wherever she goes.'

Dee sniggered. 'You have a *queen* in your universe?'

'You don't?'

'Have you got princes and princesses and dragons too?'

'We have some of those things.'

'You're winding me up.'

'Hang on, shh,' Tim whispered. There was a noise coming from outside the window. 'What the hell is that?' he asked, staring at the table they had used to block the glass.

Turning his head to listen, Tim stepped tentatively

towards the sound. He arrived at the window and very gently edged the table sideways to look. A sharp light dazzled his eyes, then metallic commotion outside made him flinch. It was a drone – hovering there, its scanning search beam locked on to them now.

'No,' Tim yelled, shoving the table back. 'How? How did they find us? We were so careful, we—' Then he saw it, stuck on the side of the imagination box: a small black gadget. 'A tracking device,' he said. They must have put it on in the helicopter. 'We led them straight here.'

'That's why the guards on the train let us go,' Dee said quietly. 'Not because they didn't recognise us, but because they did.'

There was a crunching sound: glass shattered and the window frame splintered as the drone bashed the table, trying to get inside. Before Tim could get his weight against it, the machine made it through and was right there, right in the room, looming large and loud. Its wild searchlight sent black shadows up the wall and a taser fizzled blue on the end of a stick.

A brutal zap and a bolt of what looked like

lightning hit Tim on the shoulder, sending him flat. Spinning and wobbling, the ceiling seemed to drift away, the walls too. Dazed, he rolled on to his side and heard people wrestling against the furniture in the doorway – stomping boots and angry voices. An electric shock had put Tim on the ground, but it was the weight of fear that kept him there.

Room ninety-eight, the only safe place, had fallen.

Chapter 16

It took Tim a few seconds to find his balance after that drone, which was still hovering above thanks to the technological innovations of Whitelock Industries, tasered him. His shoulder was full of hot ache and he could smell burnt hair. He remembered feeling sorry for the one they'd smashed in the field – he had seen no similar sympathy from *this* nasty hunk of metal.

Dee was throwing things at it. Eisenstone was jabbing it away with a tall lamp Tim had made. However Phil had taken matters into his own hands, scurrying up a stack of chairs and diving on top of the buzzing machine – he disappeared in through a small vent at the back.

A moment later the round drone seemed to vomit

sparks with a flash of yellow. Then it clattered to the ground, its searchlight spinning like a Catherine wheel. Phil emerged triumphantly on to the outer casing and spat out a tiny mouthful of circuitry.

'Sharp teeth,' the monkey said, grinning.

'Nice job,' Tim added, sitting up.

To his right, however, the furniture blockade in the doorway was shuffling and banging as a group of armed Grey Guards continued to break their way through.

The professor crouched by his side. 'Tim, listen,' he said. 'Run. Run and find the imagination station – do whatever it takes. You know, in, in your heart.' He touched Tim's chest. 'You know what needs to happen. You have to undo it. You have to *undo it all*.'

'I . . . I don't . . .'

Eisenstone flipped Tim's imagination box over, so the opening was face down on the floor. 'Go,' he said.

And then the professor slammed his back against the upturned tables in the doorway, trying to hold them in place. He looked so flimsy and old, bouncing forwards when the guards pushed, but returning each time.

'We can't leave you,' Tim said.

'What's …' he groaned, stumbling a little, 'what's the alternative?' His smart shoes were sliding now.

'He's right,' Dee said, pointing down. 'It's the only option.'

Phil agreed and scurried up into Tim's shirt pocket. As he got to his feet, Tim straightened his reader hat, closed his eyes and imagined pure energy, heat – a concentrated beam of power. *Power* – it roared red in his mind. The upside-down imagination box vibrated, and then smoke bellowed out from underneath. It sunk a little into the floorboards, then fell through completely, leaving a rough, smouldering hole. Tim looked down – the room below was occupied by an understandably startled couple who had pulled the covers up over themselves and huddled near the headboard. At the foot of the bed, plaster and paint flakes and dust covered everything, including the cube of metal which had come inexplicably through their ceiling.

Tim lowered himself down first, landing clumsily on the mattress. 'Evening,' he said.

The couple were stunned, glancing up at the damage and back to him. Just as the man began to speak, Dee came falling in, bouncing off the corner of the bed and crashing head first into the wardrobe door, smashing it off its hinges.

'Uh, that's higher than it looks,' she said, composing herself.

'Sorry about all this,' Tim added. 'Ask for a refund. Elisa Green's the manager – she's actually quite a nice person really.'

They went to the door but heard voices outside. 'Let's keep going down,' Dee suggested.

So he flipped the box over again and they blasted their way through a few more floors, leaving a surprisingly high tunnel above them in their wake. However, before the final attempt, Tim realised they had coincidently landed in a very special place. His room. Or, rather, the room that *should* be his.

It was empty and horribly clean. He stood for a moment, remembering how it used to be. How he'd customised it – how he'd made a home, added character to what would normally be a boring and uniform environment. That was the beauty of it. That's what made it so special. Just like room ninety-eight. This thought made Tim angry, furious with everything – particularly himself. Why had he chosen to hide *here* of all places? How could he have been so stupid?

'Tim, come on. What are you ... Tim, stop it, stop it!' Dee yelled.

Coming to his senses, Tim realised that the imagination box was on its side and oozing with bubbling lava. Orange flames licked around everything the glowing liquid touched. The corner of the machine was black, half-melted.

'Water,' Phil yelled from Tim's top pocket. 'Think of water.'

'Wait, stop, shh.' Tim could only see red. He crouched and grabbed his head, trying to calm down. 'Water, water,' he whispered to himself.

It helped to be vivid, so Tim swam through his memories – all the ones which featured water. A thirsty glug on a hot summer's day. That sudden noise the shower makes when it comes on. The ocean creeping up a still beach. Seaweed tickling your ankles. Slippery rocks. Rain. He opened his eyes. Still, all he saw was fire. Half the room was alight now, smoke collecting on the ceiling and disappearing up the makeshift chimney they'd jumped through.

Another water memory – something specific, come on. Eisenstone explaining the remarkable nature of the physical world. Elements mixed together create incredible things. Take sodium and chlorine, for example. Both dangerous chemicals. Combine them to make sodium chloride and you've got common table salt. Indeed. And what about water? Well that's made of oxygen and hydrogen. Two parts hydrogen, one part oxygen. 'H2O,' Tim yelled to himself.

There was a bang.

The imagination box flew straight out the window, spinning off the frame and disappearing outside. A fierce blaze around the bed now and Tim and Dee were getting back to their feet, both with blackened faces.

'That was *not* water,' Dee said, wiping soot from her cheek.

'Hydrogen,' Tim groaned. 'I think I managed that part.'

'Quite the explosive element,' Phil added.

They made it downstairs, running amid a panicked group of hotel guests. The building was evacuating and quite rightly so – the fire was well out of control. Everywhere he went, Tim thought to himself as they ran through the lobby, there was nothing but chaos.

Outside there were police cars and a Grey Guard armoured vehicle on the street – there to arrest them. Luckily the officers were busy with crowd control. So Tim and Dee ran round into the alleyway and retrieved the imagination box. Charred and partly melted, the metalwork looked like someone had practised welding on it. There were dents from its falls, the lid was long gone and every side was covered in scratches.

They went to the next street, then doubled back on themselves. The road outside the hotel was heaving. The fire brigade had arrived. They were unravelling a hose and pointing and running the opposite way to everyone else. Eisenstone was thankfully outside. He was however in handcuffs and being lowered into the back of a police car.

For a few minutes Tim and Dee stood and watched the drama. And then Tim spotted Elisa. There, beneath a lamppost, she was crying. Beyond all of this, the Dawn Star Hotel stood proud. Proud, but burning.

'Destroying things is too easy,' Tim whispered to himself.

It was late, probably gone midnight, Tim guessed. He and Dee's fleeing had brought them through Glassbridge, through the park and, again, they found themselves in the dark of the fields. No more street lights out here – just open countryside. Tim noticed that the further you went from the glare of the town, the more stars you could see above. Hundreds and hundreds of little white dots.

Looking back down, he realised he was standing completely still.

'Hurry,' Dee said from up ahead – he couldn't see her though.

'Why?' Tim asked. 'Where are we even going?'

'We're running,' she said. 'That's what Granddad told us to do.'

Behind, above the hotel, there was still a thick haze of smoke glowing in the night.

'I'm sick of running.'

'Look, they've arrested him,' Dee said. 'You said yourself that Clarice will kill to keep her secret. If not for your own problems, help me find the imagination station to save his life.'

Before tonight's events, Tim was relentlessly optimistic. He had so much faith in his own abilities. Even at his lowest points, when success seemed impossible – when he was falling to his death from a crane, or diving away from helicopter blades, or dodging deadly swipes from a sabre-toothed tiger – Tim believed, deep down, that he would ultimately win. Phil had even said it – despite everything, things *always* worked out in the end.

But now? Now Tim truly believed that they might not. Maybe he *wasn't* capable of solving this one. Maybe winning just wasn't an option. Maybe this nightmare was his new home.

'What if I can't do it? What if I can't create? What if I can only destroy?'

'Come on,' Dee said. 'You've made all sorts of stuff.'

'You conjured me,' Phil added. 'Twice. Both resounding successes if I do say so myself.'

'But it's all flawed in some way,' Tim said. 'My imagination is at best inconsistent, at worst it's … it's dangerous.'

'So, what are you saying?' Dee asked.

'I … I might not be able to use the imagination station. Even if we *did* find it. If I can't imagine water, how can I imagine a new reality? What if we're stuck here, Dee, what if we're trapped here for the rest of our lives?'

'*Trapped* here?' Dee said, raising her voice slightly. Although she was speaking from near pitch dark, Tim could tell she had turned to face him. 'I haven't even *seen* the things you're always talking about. *Here* is all I've ever known. *This* is the only reality for me. This air we're breathing, this dirt we're walking on.' She kicked some dried earth towards him. 'This is real. I can barely even *comprehend* the idea that there could be other universes. And this one – this life – has been absolutely ruined.'

'I—'

'What's more, it's almost *entirely* your fault.' Dee sounded angry. Tim had never, ever seen her lose her temper. His heart was pumping – he felt the same anxiety you get from being told off when you're small. 'So if you're hinting, even a tiny bit, that you might be thinking about giving up ... well.' She let out a deep breath. 'Let's just say that it's *not* all right. So, I'll try again ... Let's go and sort this out.'

'Uh, yeah,' Tim said, feeling oddly energised again. 'OK. Sorry. Had a bit of a wobble there.'

They found a small clearing in the woods where they positioned the imagination box (which, remarkably, still worked despite the damage) on the ground and Tim imagined gentle warmth to emerge from the top. 'No more fires,' he said.

A tiny lamp lit the opening of the tent Tim made and they all sat cross-legged in a circle and ate and drank and whispered in the night.

'OK,' Dee said after a while. 'Let's beeline for

solution boulevard. *How* can we get close enough to Clarice to extract the whereabouts of the imagination station?'

'One would suspect it is a trifle tricky to even know her location, let alone orchestrate such endeavours,' Phil said, pacing on the ground between them, one arm across his chest, his hand resting on his chin. 'Perhaps we should consider attributes of her character generally – Dee, in a sense, you are more familiar with Clarice than us. What can we say about her?'

'*What can we say about her?*' Tim repeated, lifting a finger as an idea sprouted in his mind. 'Now there's a thought. She cares about her image, right? Always doing charity stuff, trying to *look* good. Hours after we break into Crowfield Tower, she's on the ten o'clock news telling everyone it's under control?'

'So, what are you suggesting?' Dee asked.

'We need to do what we do best.'

'Which is?'

'Cause an enormous amount of trouble ...'

Chapter 17

Rows and rows of small, metal drones were lined up in the woods, all waiting to be activated. The first glints of a reddish sunrise were bathing them in an almost sepia tint – a rich warmth that seemed alive in every speck of dew on every leaf and petal. Morning birds had been performing in the canopy above for hours now. Already, it was a beautiful day.

'Proper what now?' Tim said.

Dee had been explaining her part of the idea.

'Propaganda,' she repeated. 'They do it in wars – you fly over an area and drop a load of leaflets dissing the enemy's leader, or praising yours. Or saying something or other.'

'Saying what though?'

'Anything,' Dee said. 'Use your imagination.'

They had stayed up all night putting this plan together and now almost everything was in place. The army of automated flying machines was finished – all they had left to do was load them up. Tim had copied the design of the Whitelock Industries' police drones fairly closely, but made minor tweaks. His were slightly smaller for a start and he'd also included little clips on the underside of each, which were attached to small containers about the size of shoeboxes. They looked a bit like miniature hot-air balloons made from metal.

And, as they were arranged in a fairly neat grid – each little contraption passing its long morning shadow on to the one by its side – Tim was able to count them quickly. 'Wow, there's 199 here.'

'What an annoying number,' Dee said.

Tim created one more, then set it down on the mulched woodland floor. 'Better?'

'A bit.'

'Right, now, what should we say?' Tim asked.

The idea was to drop leaflets all over London. On

the front of each would be something about Clarice. Something bad. Their thinking was: if enough rained down, people would get talking. It'd be on the news, in the papers. If it was a high-profile incident, then Clarice would *have* to go on TV to defend herself – in all likelihood she'd go on Black Feather News again (Tim wasn't surprised to hear that even TV shows had some reference to her). After all, she was on the ropes from all the chaos they'd already caused. Getting into a television studio to ambush her, they'd concluded, seemed relatively doable.

But first they had to make some leaflets. Tim, wearing his reader hat, stared into the broken, battered and bruised imagination box. Now, without a lid, you could look down into the square opening and watch the item you were creating appear, as if from nowhere. This was something Dee did with fascination.

Sure enough a piece of glossy A5 paper materialised inside the cube. Frowning, Dee lifted it out and read aloud: 'Clarice Crowfield punches puppies?'

Tim was standing with his arms proudly folded.

'That is—'

'Scandalous? Inspired?' Tim said.

'No ... more like—'

'You wanna change the wording? I like the alliteration though. Decks dogs? Kicks kittens? I just think puppies are sympathetic. Look at its little face.'

Tim had included a photo of the cutest puppy he could imagine, looking up from the leaflet with eyes like, well, like a puppy dog.

'Is it believable though?' Dee said. 'I mean, why on earth would someone punch a puppy? They're too low down, you'd have to crouch. It's impractical. Plus, she has, like, five pet dogs herself – she loves them.'

'*Exactly*. So she'll definitely want to set the record straight. Maybe we should add, "For lols" at the bottom?'

'Perhaps a stride too wide,' Phil said. 'It is already quite the defamatory accusation.'

And so they loaded up the drones, one by one, with well over a hundred flyers each.

'Is that enough?' Tim wondered.

'A hundred times two hundred? That's what?' Dee closed her eyes for a second.

'Millions,' Tim said.

'It's loads,' she agreed, waving her hand.

As they were preprogrammed, Tim stepped back to a single control switch he had created and flicked it on. There was a surprisingly loud, electronic buzz as every drone came alive and lifted into the air, kicking up a little dust. A startled rabbit, which had been milling about, bolted off into a nearby bush. Clever enough not to bump into each other, the army of drones all hovered gently and found their own space about a metre off the ground.

Tim felt powerful, like a conductor, as he raised an arm and flicked another button. Then, like paper lanterns set free, they drifted up and away effortlessly in an expanding crowd. One, two, three, four, then more, stuttered and fell heavily out of the sky, thudding to the ground. Tim shrugged and said, 'Bound to be a few defects here and there.'

Within a minute the drones looked like a flock of birds above the treetops and then, a minute after that, they were so far away and so spread out they were invisible.

'I'm excited,' Tim said, smiling in the early sun. 'Even if this plan fails, it's still proper funny.'

It happened quicker than they expected. Checking their phones, Tim and Dee saw that by noon every single news website was reporting the outrageous (and hilarious) accusation that Clarice Crowfield – the *Prime Minister of the Great British Empire* – punches puppies. There was footage of hundreds of leaflets raining down over London, swinging and spinning from the sky like autumn leaves, Crowfield Tower still closed off in the backdrop. Some news sites were describing it as a prank, others as a serious public disturbance. There was even the word 'terrorism' knocking about. At any rate, it was working.

'This is amazing,' Dee said, reading the coverage.

Next Tim created a very special drone – one which he really concentrated on. This particular one had to be safe as it would have a pilot.

'Hang on, does that mean it's not a drone, if it's manned?' Dee wondered.

'Technically it's not manned, it's monkeyed,' Tim said. 'Right, Phil. Are you ready?'

'Aye aye, captain,' Phil said, clambering into the small contraption.

It had wings and a cockpit – it looked a bit like a model of a futuristic fighter jet, capable of full flight *and* hovering.

'Now it's programmed by GPS to go straight to Black Feather Studios – it should just land on the roof. But, if you run into trouble, the manual controls are here, and here.' Tim pointed at a small stick and button console.

He then opened a small hatch on the back and dropped in an orange teleportation sphere (about the size of a golf ball). The blue counterpart was safely tucked away in his pocket. Tim had to reassure Dee that teleportation technology was relatively safe and something he had experience in. However, although he paid special attention when making these items, there was a slight fear in his stomach that they might be faulty. The consequences of a malfunctioning teleportation ball didn't bear thinking about. It'd probably result in some terrible disfigurement. Or, perhaps more unsettling, you'd disappear but never reappear. You'd simply be gone.

'Make sure you leave the sphere somewhere with a bit of space too,' Tim added. 'No good us teleporting into a wall cavity and suffocating.'

'Right you are.'

'I've also made you a miniature phone, with my number saved on it,' Tim said. The mobile was about half the size of a postage stamp. 'Give us a text when you're in.'

'Yes, yes.'

'And Phil,' Tim said, 'be careful because I've built in a—'

'Oh, fret not, Timothy,' the monkey said, straightening his tiny leather pilot's goggles. 'I have everything under control. Lift off!'

Phil slammed a hand on to a button and, with a bang, disappeared straight up into the air, his scream fading quickly to silence. The flying contraption, however, was still in the same place on the ground – the monkey had, in fact, hit the eject switch.

Around thirty seconds later he came floating down in a small parachute. 'You were saying?' Phil asked casually, as he landed.

Having been clipped back into place and properly briefed, Phil took off successfully and zipped away into the afternoon sky.

Later, Tim packed the imagination box into his rucksack and prepared himself. It had been almost two hours since Phil left and they began discussing all the things that might have gone wrong. However, finally, Tim's mobile buzzed in his pocket. He had a text message from the monkey which read:

Dearest Timothy and Dee,

I understand that this medium of communication suffers conventions, frankly approaching philistinism, which see users shortening words or even, would you believe, substituting them entirely with single letters. But there shall be no such erosion of proper English from me. No, sir. Furthermore, I note that these telecommunication corporations insist on moving us ever closer to a plausibly harrowing dystopia in which all words are replaced by illustrations of basic emotions. The 'emoji' is a curious notion and one that instils in me an impalpable malaise. While some of these are fun ... Actually, they are great. I just had a look at them. Oh my, there's one with a frog. Hahaha, froggy frog face. Lord, these are brilliant. A pinecone! There's a whole page of cat ones.

'Is that all a single text message?' Dee asked, peering down at the phone.

'Yeah, it's about five pages long.' Tim scrolled through, skipping much of the rambling.

... and so, there we have it. The common
ostrich cannot fly, but it *can* swim.
Perhaps more fish than bird?

'That's the end of the message?' Tim said. 'God,
he's forgotten what he's supposed to be doing. He's
probably ended up—'

Another text buzzed into the phone. Tim
opened it:

Oh, btw, have arrived @ TV studios,
broke in through air-con unit and
put teleportation ball thingy on a
table in back room. See you soon, lots
of love, Phil the Finger Monkey xx

'Right, you ready?' Tim put his arm around Dee
and held the teleportation sphere in front of them.

'You *sure* this will work?' she asked. 'I don't want to
end up fifty feet in the air or something.'

Tim swallowed – he hadn't even thought of that

possibility. 'I'm sure-ish,' he said, breathing in some courage. 'Sure enough to do *this*.'

He clicked the button and, with a short, harsh whistle-zip, they disappeared – some dried mud curled in the air where they'd been but, besides that, they were gone.

A rebirth – a startled gasping breath as they re-emerged at the other end. Tim patted himself down, making sure all his limbs had arrived. Dee too was checking herself over.

'It worked,' she whispered. Another seemingly impossible thing had just happened to her. To think, her life was completely normal a few days ago.

Setting down the orange teleportation sphere, Tim took in the surroundings. This was a large dressing room. A huge black feather logo was emblazoned on the wall. Near that were racks of costumes and a curtained-off area. It was silent, besides one sound – a strange, quiet singing. On the other side of the room was a large mirror, surrounded by golden glowing light bulbs. And in front of it was a finger monkey, walking up and down as though on a catwalk or something, all the while humming to himself.

'La, la, la dee daaaah,' he sang, with each strut. 'A dah, dee-dah, dee-dah.'

Then he stopped, flung back his head as though he had long hair and looked at his own reflection, still yet to notice Tim and Dee.

Phil was turning and admiring himself from different angles, like a model. 'Being invited to the Simian Oscars is honour enough,' he said to himself. 'But to win Best Monkey is a dream come true. I wish to thank everyone who has believed in me and sup—'

He stopped dead, spotting Tim and Dee in the mirror, standing behind him.

'How long have you been there?' he said.

'Long enough,' Dee replied.

'Are you wearing make-up?' Tim asked.

'Am I wearing make-up?' Phil chuckled a few times, then straightened his face. 'Maybe.'

Dee approached an open wardrobe, and put on a bowler hat and a fluffy bright green scarf. She slid her hands into long leather gloves then looked through the clothes.

'Some of this is great,' she said. 'Would it be wrong to steal— Hello, pirate costume.'

A pirate hat came spinning over her shoulder. Tim caught it. 'No, stop,' he said, but still put it on his head over his beanie. 'This is a big building. We have to work out where Clarice will be.'

'Oh, I sorted that out,' Phil said. 'I looked on the register when I broke in. Headline guest on the six o'clock news is none other than Clarice Crowfield.'

'That's good,' Dee said, opening a large make-up box.

It amazed Tim how calm she was at a time like this. 'Why aren't you more concerned?'

'Look.' She turned to him, holding a small brush in a slack hand. 'They've arrested Granddad – that's a problem. Can I solve it at this precise moment in time? No. So what good would it do to get all anxious about it?'

'You can't just choose how you feel,' Tim said with, a sigh. 'That's not how emotions work.'

'Yeah but it is.'

'Besides, we still need to sort out a plan for Clarice,' Tim added. 'She won't just *tell us* where the imagination station is.'

'Truth serum,' Dee said, putting lipstick on in the mirror now. 'Tranquiliser-type gun, shoot her in the neck, bam, done.'

'I'm worried it'll kill her,' Tim said.

'Timothy raises a sound point,' Phil added. 'The ethics of administering home-made drugs intravenously to unwilling recipients are colourful to say the least.'

'Just really concentrate,' Dee said. 'Make sure the serum isn't actually jam or bleach – give it some real thought.'

'Fine,' Tim said. 'But that still doesn't cover how we get close enough to her.'

'Oh, do not worry about *that*,' Phil added. 'This is the VIP dressing room. I overheard two producers saying she would be coming in here – they cleaned it especially.'

Tim glared. 'So, she'll be here, what, soon?'

'I would imagine so,' Phil said. 'It is gone half past five.'

'OK,' Tim said, his heart pumping, his breath picking up. He was trying not to think about how scared he was. 'I'm scared,' he heard himself say, which didn't help. 'Let's find somewhere to—'

A sound. Someone was outside the room. The door handle was turning. Tim and Dee made panicked eye contact as it swung open and a man entered.

They hid inside the costume wardrobe – the door resting silently closed – just in time. It was dark in there and the old fabric smelled of lofts and dust. Through a small slit, Tim watched the man have a casual look around the room. He checked under the dressing mirror, then peered along the floor a bit. As he was wearing a black suit, a curly wire earpiece and black sunglasses, Tim guessed he was a bodyguard. The man stopped and noticed the closet, seemingly staring right into Tim's eyes hidden inside. They pulled costumes in front of themselves and tensed against the back wall. Oblivious, the man opened the door and, after a terrible five-second pause, closed it again.

'All clear,' the man said into a radio in his sleeve as he perched on the edge of the table.

And then Tim's heart fell silent and his lungs sat still as Clarice Crowfield stepped inside the dressing room.

Chapter 18

'I just don't understand,' Clarice said, sitting on the chair in front of the mirror.

'Nothing to understand, ma'am,' the bodyguard replied. 'It's no more than some crazy folk with too much time on their hands.'

Safely hidden in the dusty costume closet, Tim could lean left and right to see more of the dressing room. The border of golden bulbs around the mirror in front of Clarice lit her well – she actually looked quite pretty, Tim thought. Which was weird. And her voice too, like last night at the charity dinner, sounded softer than he remembered.

'It's ...' Clarice said. 'It's just such an extraordinary thing to have to deny.'

'We'll find 'em,' the man added.

'I hope so.' She sighed.

The plan had been to shoot Clarice with a dart containing truth serum. However, that scheme would now be difficult as the imagination box was on the other side of the room. Tim had had time to get it out of the rucksack, but he hadn't had time to create anything, least of all a tranquiliser gun. Honestly, he was half relieved, because shooting the Prime Minister with a drugged dart was another thing he could imagine a judge reading out in court. It just *sounds* bad.

But, still, now they were close to her. Close enough to strike. To … to do something. And yet Tim couldn't think what – his mind was in a frantic rush.

'What are we going to do?' Dee whispered.

Clarice was checking her long, straight black hair in the mirror and—

'Oh no,' Tim whispered back, spotting the bodyguard stepping towards the imagination box.

'What the hell is this thing?' the man said, crouching next to it.

'Whatever it is,' Clarice replied, fiddling with an earring, 'it's broken.'

'Yeah, right,' the man said. 'Look at the state of it.'

'Timothy,' Phil whispered from Tim's top pocket, 'I have some extremely bad news.'

'What?'

'I . . . I think I am about to sneeze.'

'You must not sneeze,' Dee whispered. 'That must not happen.'

'It is happening,' the monkey said in a rising high-pitched voice.

'No.' Tim put a hand over Phil's face. Still, the tiny sneeze was loud enough for both Clarice and the bodyguard to stop and turn their attention to the large wardrobe.

'It has happened,' Phil whispered with a sniff. 'How are things looking now?'

'Very terrible,' Tim said.

'We know you're in there,' the bodyguard yelled. 'Step out *slowly*.'

'It sounds like they have found us,' Phil whispered. 'We are just going to have to stay in here forever.'

'You can't stay in there forever,' the man added.

'Damn.'

'Tim, I hope you've got a good plan,' Dee said.

And then she pushed open the door and they both stepped out. Two guilty-looking children, both in various stages of fancy dress. Tim noticed then that Phil was no longer in his pocket.

The bodyguard had a gun, which was pointing at the floor. However, the second he recognised them, he lifted it. 'Ma'am, get behind me,' he said, standing large and bold.

'Relax,' Clarice said, gently placing her hand on the pistol and pushing it down. 'They're just children.'

All at once Tim had a thousand ideas. He was still wearing his reader hat and the imagination box was on the other side of the room, without a lid. There *had* to be a way out of this, he thought, considering the infinite number of things he could create. From long robotic arms equipped with restraints, to a cloud of sleeping gas – from a plague of locusts, to an elaborate tentacle life form that would emerge and snatch that gun from the bodyguard's hand. He even considered

239

things that wouldn't help them even slightly, such as a sentient pineapple or an extremely aggressive swarm of death hornets. Murder bees. Psycho wasps.

All these options and he picked, drumroll, nothing. Yep. He just stood there, frozen. Frozen by fear and confusion. Mostly by fear.

'Tim,' Dee whispered from the side of her mouth. 'Gonna need that solution ASAP.'

Clarice stepped forwards. 'It's all right,' she said over her shoulder when her bodyguard protested. 'What were you doing in there?' she asked them.

'Hiding,' Dee said. 'I mean, it's the only place *to* hide in here, so you should sack him for a start.' She pointed at the bodyguard, who frowned.

'*Why* were you hiding in there?' Clarice asked.

She had arrived in front of Tim and crouched, so her eyes were lower than his. He was still unable to do anything, unable to create, unable to move. But, steadily, something strange began to happen. The fear drained away. There was something in Clarice's eyes that comforted him. She truly meant no harm. If anything, instead of anger, there was kindness in her face. *Clarice Crowfield*, a woman Tim had assumed was irretrievably evil, looked like she was worried for him.

'We ... we came to see you,' Tim said.

'Why?'

'Because ...' He glanced at Dee and found a little bolt of confidence. 'Because we know what you did.'

'I assure you, young man, I have *never* punched a—'

'No, not that. Rick Harris. The imagination station. Ring any bells?'

'The ... what?'

'Don't play dumb,' Tim said, trying to sound surer and braver than he felt. 'You stole the imagination station from TRAD and created all of *this*. This crazy world of yours where you're Prime Minister and everyone loves you. It's all a lie.'

Clarice took Tim's hand and cupped it in hers, then slightly shook her head. 'Is this why you broke into Crowfield Tower? It's OK,' she whispered. 'Sometimes a troubled mind can play tricks on you. Things can seem real when they're not.'

For a moment he felt completely safe. In a strange

way he kind of wanted to hug her. She had that slightly glazy warmth he'd only ever seen once before, in Elisa's eyes. But then he snapped out of it and snatched his hand away.

'Stop, I know the truth,' he said, speaking fast. 'You kidnapped Professor Eisenstone. You accidently created a *monster* that destroyed your house. That was the contents of your mind, of your personality. *That* is what you are.'

'W-what are you talking—'

'You had Fredric Wilde killed, and blamed it on us,' Dee added.

'No, no—'

'You tormented your own son,' Tim went on. 'I saw his memories. I saw how you treated him. You blamed him – his birth – for all *your* failings. You *hated* Stephen. You *hated* everyone.'

'That's not—'

'And he hated you,' Tim whispered.

'Listen to me,' Clarice said in a firm but caring voice. 'There has been a lot of crazy stuff said about me, but one thing I can tell you for *sure* is that I don't hate Stephen. I love him, he's the … the apple of my eye, my inspiration. His birth was the happiest day of my life. Everything I've ever done, has been for him.'

It was possible that Clarice had erased her own memories – maybe she didn't want to remember how she got to where she was. But surely there was no way she would make herself so fond of Stephen?

'I don't understand,' Tim said. 'I … I just …'

However, then, like a forgotten name sailing home to your mind, it was so clear and so obvious. Of course, Tim thought to himself, feeling frustrated that he hadn't figured it out sooner.

'It's not her,' Dee whispered, realising it herself.

'This isn't the world *you* want,' Tim said, his eyes scrunched in defeat. 'It's the world Stephen wants.'

'What?' Clarice was still just as confused.

'It's your son we're after,' Tim explained, thinking aloud. 'He stole the imagination station. *He* changed everything. And … and he gave you all you've ever wished for, even after everything you did to him … All he wanted was a happy mother who would love him.'

Sighing, Tim laughed to himself. He had to. It was either laughing or crying.

'Where is Stephen?' Dee asked. Her eyes were still very much on the prize.

'I suspect he's at his home, or at GGHQ.'

'GGHQ? What does he do?' Dee said.

'He's . . . he's in charge of the Grey Guards,' Clarice said. 'Why does it matter?'

'What about George Eisenstone?' Dee asked. 'Where is he?'

'I don't know.'

'Listen,' Tim said, staring into Clarice's eyes. 'We need to go and speak to Stephen.'

'Young man,' she said, tilting his pirate hat back. 'They say I have a heart of gold, but even my tolerance has its limits. This is the end of your exploits.'

Tim stepped back, towards the door.

'Ah, no,' the bodyguard said, grabbing him. 'You kids aren't going anywhere.' He looked down at Tim. 'Why are you wearing two hats?' And, before Tim could use creativity to escape, both his pirate hat and reader beanie were whisked off his head. Then the man lifted his wrist to his face and said into his hidden radio, 'Agent C6, Unit 2. I need immediate backup in the VIP green room at Black Feather Studios. I have Timothy Hart and Dee Eisenstone in custody.'

The dressing room was full of people within a minute. Tim and Dee were in handcuffs and being told they were in an enormous amount of trouble. They just listened and nodded. As Phil was still hidden in that costume wardrobe, Tim made a special effort not to look at it.

One of the police officers who had arrived spoke with the bodyguard near the door.

'Security level five, eh?' the policeman said. 'What does that actually mean?'

'Who knows?' The bodyguard shrugged. 'But, if we lose 'em again, we're all out of a job. So take 'em somewhere *secure* and quiet for now and wait for further orders from GGHQ.'

'There's only one place for you then,' the policeman said before throwing a mean smile Tim's way. 'You guys familiar with a place called Hawk Peak Prison?'

Chapter 19

The tall metal door slammed shut and a loud lock clacked into place. Then an electronic mechanism clamped with a buzzing sound.

'I really do think we should be able to speak to a lawyer or something,' Dee said through the bars.

There was no response. Instead, the prison guard just whistled and strolled off up the corridor, his truncheon scratching along the walls and echoing off each metal door as he went.

When he was gone, all Tim could hear was a pipe trickling somewhere outside. *Drip. Drip. Drip.*

He sat on the mattress and cupped his head in his hands. The police had driven them here in the back of a van and shoved them roughly inside. Usually Tim would have used the fact that he was a child to get a bit of slack. But after everything they'd done, it seemed the police weren't feeling particularly sympathetic. And, after all, they were working for Stephen Crowfield – following his orders, carrying out his bidding.

Drip. Drip. Drip.

That nervous young man Tim remembered popped into his mind. He assumed Stephen had stolen the imagination station and then, instead of handing it over to his mother, decided to use it himself. Maybe he realised what damage she might do. Maybe this *was* the lesser of two evils.

Tim had always felt sorry for Stephen – he wasn't a bad guy, really, at heart. He was a victim of his mother – every wrong thing he'd ever done was because of her. If anything, having seen Stephen make Clarice disappear in her teleporter, Tim thought of him more as an ally than an enemy. Of course, Stephen couldn't have known at the time that Rick Harris would later *fix* the device and effectively bring Clarice back from the dead. As far as he was concerned, he was killing her.

'I always thought of Stephen as a good person,' Tim said, thinking aloud. He was having to change his entire opinion of the man. 'But ... he pretty much murdered his own mother.'

'In the broken teleporter?'

'Yeah.'

'But you said she abused him his whole life?' Dee added.

'I'm not a fan of Clarice,' Tim said. 'But is death a fair punishment?'

'Whole family are nutjobs,' Dee said. 'That's all we can say for sure.'

So, as well as fear and sadness, Tim was filled with curiosity. He desperately wanted to ask Stephen *why* he'd made the universe this way – why he'd created a world where Tim's friends and family didn't recognise him. Where he was totally alone again. Why would *Stephen* want to punish him?

'Well, anyway,' Dee said, glancing around their gloomy, narrow cell with her hands on her hips. 'Here we are. Remember what I said last night, in the field?'

'Which bit?' Tim asked.

'The bit about getting annoyed if you were giving up.'

'Oh yeah.'

'*Now* would be a reasonable time to say something negative. About this being hopeless ... if you fancy it?'

'I'd rather not,' Tim said. Although he had to admit, if Dee thought things were bad, they were probably worse.

'Suit yourself. I will then. We are completely ruined. Done. It's over.' Dee tutted and sighed, but not with any real emotion. It was more the kind of sigh you do when you realise all the best flavours are gone from a box of chocolates. 'Yep.'

Tim stepped to the tiny window, near the ceiling – there were thick bars on the inside *and* the outside – but all he could really see was another brick wall. If he arched his head, he could almost see the sky, but not quite. 'Phil's still out there, somewhere.'

It seemed silly, but he imagined how Phil would handle himself if he had to live alone in the wild. He had visions of him trying to negotiate the sale of nuts with a squirrel, or naively knocking on a beehive to politely ask for some honey. Tim hadn't meant to, but he had created a creature that couldn't fit into the animal kingdom, or live a normal human life. A being without a home. The idea that Phil could get hurt, or worse die, made Tim's chest ache. Not just from grief, but because ultimately it would be his fault. Elisa was right: he really *was* responsible for Phil.

'Hmm, yeah,' Dee said. 'But this is Hawk Peak Prison. As much as I love that furry little guy, I somehow doubt he can bust us out of here.'

'Hey, kiddies,' a creepy voice said from a nearby cell. 'Hey, kiddieeeees.'

'It really is not OK to lock us up in an adult prison,' Dee said.

'Hey, kiddies,' the croaky voice yelled again.

'Shut up,' Dee yelled back through the door hatch. 'We don't want to be your friend.'

'Why not?' The man sounded genuinely hurt by that remark.

'That's what you've got to do in prison,' Dee whispered to Tim. 'Be hard. Don't take any nonsense.

Or they'll shove you about, steal your porridge and probably do worse stuff too.'

'You know that's old Wild Freddie's cell,' the voice said.

He was referring to Fredric Wilde. Glancing around Tim realised this was, indeed, Fredric's cell. He had an eerie feeling when he saw the 'NO MUSIC' sign on the wall. What a mean-spirited punishment, he thought again, to ban *music*. The only melody they had was that infuriating *drip, drip, drip* of water outside.

'They made him disappear,' the man shouted. 'That's what happens here. People come in, but ain't no one gets out. You hear me?' He sounded insane. 'No one gets out of Hawk Peak!' He laughed.

The guard appeared at their door. 'Change of plans,' he said. 'You kids are getting transferred. Transport will be here in an hour.'

'Oh,' the crazy man said. 'Well, *usually* no one gets out.'

Again, the guard wandered off.

'Transferred where, I wonder?' Dee said.

'To a graveyard?' Tim replied. 'And in an hour? Why not wait until the morning? It's the middle of the night.'

Drip-drip, drip-drip. It was getting faster now.

'You kids like cabbage?' the voice said again.

'Leave 'em alone,' another inmate shouted. 'Just ignore Stabby Pete – he's always mean to new faces.'

These different voices came echoing down the hall – Tim couldn't be sure how many prisoners were out there in this wing. For now though, only two were speaking.

'This guy sounds nicer,' Tim whispered.

'My name's Hammer,' the kinder voice said. 'End of the hall there's Screamy Joe.'

A man let out a short scream – 'Ah!' – as an introduction.

'Go away,' Dee yelled back.

'You don't need to do the tough talk,' Tim said. 'We're not staying here.'

'Still. Hammer, Screamy Joe, *Stabby Pete*?' Dee said. 'These don't sound like the kind of people you invite round for dinner.'

'You know there's a place downstairs,' Stabby Pete said again in his taunting voice. 'A place no one's allowed to go. If you ask about it, you get a week in solitary. Rumour has it, that's where they send people. Down into the secret, dark hole. Maybe *that's* where you're being transferred. Ain't no one knows what happens in there. But I'm guessing it ain't good.'

'Mr Stabby, Pete, whatever your name is,' Dee said back. 'We know you're just trying to scare us. Grow up, mate.'

'I'm just tellin' you how it is.'

'Well, we don't believe you,' Dee said.

'Nah, it's true,' Hammer added. 'There is an off-limits basement, but it's nothing but a storage area – no ghosts, no nothing.'

'You don't know,' Stabby Pete yelled. 'You don't know what's down there.'

Dee sighed and sat next to Tim on the bed. 'Let's just ignore them,' she said.

The dripping was now full-flowing water, as constant as a running tap.

'It's raining,' Tim whispered, looking up at the window.

After a while, the inmates quietened down and the weather took over – a heavy storm with swinging winds and fast rain.

It was all so loud that they didn't hear a banging on the glass.

However, Tim glanced up after a particularly long round of thunder and saw a shadow. Something was moving outside on the windowsill. He leant closer. Something small. And then a vivid flash turned the frame a sudden blue and there he was – a perfect silhouette standing between the black bars.

'Phil,' Tim whispered. He tapped on Dee's shoulder. 'Look.'

They dragged the bed across the floor so they could stand on it and be at eye level with him. Even though they could tell the monkey was yelling, they couldn't hear a word he was saying over the storm's music.

Realising, he scuttled away and returned a short while later with something in his hand, a small device, which he placed on the glass. Then he pulled something over his face – a strange metal mask with a horizontal slit, the kind you wear for welding.

'Yes,' Tim whispered.

A tiny bright red laser appeared, fizzing and sparkling against the window, steam lifting away in the wet weather.

After a few seconds, a perfect coin of glass fell inside and the monkey removed his welding mask. There was a cold whistle at the hole, like air blown over an open bottle top.

'Good evening,' Phil said, poking his head through. 'Did someone order a finger monkey?'

Overjoyed to see him, Tim quickly grabbed the creature and held him in the palm of his hand. His fur was soaked through and he was shivering, his heart beating like a worried mouse.

'How did you get all the way here?' Tim asked.

'You made me a flying contraption, of course.'

'And where did you get the miniature glass-cutter weldy thing?'

'Alas, I invite you to gaze upon my most mighty wonder.' Phil leapt up and scurried back outside, then returned with a small metal cube. He placed it carefully on the windowsill.

'Is that ...' Dee leant closer to look at the tiny gadget. 'Is that an imagination box?'

'Why, yes it is,' the monkey said, puffing his chest with pride. 'You left your one in the dressing room and for the life of me I just could not decide what jailbreaking equipment I might need. The logical answer was to keep all my options open.'

'Nice one.' Tim knew Phil could use the technology too (he had created bear-sharks in the imagination space, after all), but he was still impressed to see a to-scale version of the machine. He stroked it with a careful fingertip. All the detail was there, perfectly recreated. Its reader was no larger than a thimble, the box itself the size of an ice cube – it looked like a delicate toy.

'Hang on,' Dee said, straining in thought and turning to Tim. 'The finger monkey you created in the imagination box, used an imagination box, which you created in an imagination box, to create an imagination box?'

'Exemplary summary,' Phil said. 'Akin to Russian dolls, but with cutting-edge science in lieu of curvaceous, perpetually pregnant wooden women. Fantabulous times. But listen, after you were arrested, back at the studios, I eavesdropped on one of the officers speaking to Stephen Crowfield on the telephone. I did not catch the entire conversation, but he sounded seriously perturbed – he said he was coming here *himself*. I would strongly advise you to explore options of escape.'

'Phil, this prison is renowned for being the most secure place on earth,' Dee said. 'Getting out of this cell is virtually impossible, getting out of this corridor is virtually impossible – how long would it take to cut through all those bars? Then you've got a ten-metre perimeter fence with razor wire and armed guards posted in towers. Then you've got *another* perimeter fence outside of that. Spotlights, motion sensors, CCTV, growling German shepherds chasing you – that's just the security we know is out there. And we have, like, twenty minutes.'

Phil turned to his creation. 'Hello? Imagination

box. Let us say I fabricate some kind of tunnelling device, or some sort of skeleton key, or explosives?'

'We'd need to . . .' Dee pouted. 'Teleport.'

'The teleportation sphere,' Tim said, excitedly. '*Tell me* you brought that with you.'

'Why, I collected it and put it in the rear compartment of Monkey Force One,' Phil said.

'Aw, thank God. It'll take us back to the woods,' Tim said.

'I could create another one?' Phil said, hopeful.

'No need, too risky.'

'So I made the imagination box for nothing?' The monkey was hunched like a sulking teenager.

'You cut the glass, Phil,' Tim said, trying to reassure him. 'You did well.'

'Let's just go.' Dee lifted two thumbs and danced. 'Jail, jail, jailbreak.'

'Fine. Wait here,' Phil said, clambering back up to the window hole. He scurried away, up the wall and to the roof where he'd parked his tiny jet. He returned thirty seconds or so later and passed the teleportation sphere through.

Tim literally kissed it. 'Well done, Phil, *well done*.'

This was their chance at an escape. It was one of those strokes of luck that made Tim feel dizzy to think about any other option.

They huddled close and Tim held the small gadget in his hand. Dee held it too. Phil looked on from Tim's top pocket, hugging his tiny imagination box and wearing its tiny reader – it kept falling over his eyes and he kept tilting it back. 'Ready?' Tim said.

With a triumphant breath he placed his thumb on the button and—

'Wait,' Dee said. 'Wait just one second . . .' She took the metal ball from him and placed it on the mattress. 'Why would they lock us up, only to have us taken out straight away? Why transfer us in the middle of the night? Doesn't that seem weird to you? What's the rush?'

'What are you saying?' Tim asked.

Dee narrowed her eyes. 'Remember what they said in the helicopter, before the cobra business?'

'Aw, I do miss Barry,' Phil said.

'Security level five.' Dee was frowning. She

259

began to pace. 'None of the police know who we are, or why we're *really* wanted so badly. Not even Clarice knew.'

'Well, they're just following Stephen's orders,' Tim said.

'But maybe they *weren't* ordered to lock us up *here*. They did that because they were so worried about us slipping away again.' Dee was nodding. 'And now they've been given *new orders*, from GGHQ, the Grey Guards, to have us transferred *as soon as possible*?'

'Stephen is coming here *personally*,' Phil added, leaping on to the mattress and looking up at them. 'Are my vocal cords faulty? We have to leave.'

'Exactly,' Dee said. 'We *have to leave*. Stephen doesn't want us to be here, not even for one night. We know he visited Fredric in this very prison to ask for his help – and, among other things, they talked about Hawk Peak's reputation ...' Dee glared at them both. 'If you were Stephen Crowfield, where would *you* hide the imagination station?'

Tim laughed gently. 'In the most secure place I could find,' he said, staring at the wall.

'I think,' Dee whispered, 'I think we're exactly where we need to be.'

Phil still didn't seem to have worked it out. But then, steadily, his eyes widened, his mouth fell open and he lifted a finger. 'Goodness gracious grapes and olives,' he said, pointing at Tim. '*You* still owe me a hat.'

Chapter 20

The prison cell had a steely chill, the kind of damp cold that gets in your clothes and hair – the hole in the window only made it worse.

Phil scurried up on to the pillow, then on to the corner of the bed frame where he perched like a tiny gargoyle. He was dry now – his fur had a just-washed fluff about it. 'Ever so sorry, I missed what you were saying – my mind suffers from insatiable wanderlust,' he said.

'The imagination station is *here*,' Tim explained. 'Here in Hawk Peak Prison. It's the perfect hiding place.'

'Seems an interesting theory, this being somewhat of an impenetrable fortress,' Phil replied, stroking flat the hairs on his arms. 'But, dare I say, one of significant scale.'

'Yeah, but …' Tim stood quickly and stepped to the cell door. 'Hey, Stabby Pete, Hammer,' he said through the bars. 'This secret basement …'

The other inmates explained that there was a large hatch in the middle of the open courtyard – which was explicitly off limits – and it was used to access a storage area beneath the prison. No one knew what it contained, hence the speculation and scare stories. Not even the guards had access, they said.

'Who *does* have access?' Tim said.

'Far as I know,' Hammer replied, 'only the warden's boss.'

'Who's that?' Dee asked.

'Stephen Crowfield,' Hammer said.

'You definitely heard Stephen say he was coming here?' Dee whispered to Phil.

'With my own ears,' the monkey replied.

Tim thought to himself for a moment, then rolled his eyes. 'Of course,' he said. 'He's coming to get the imagination station.'

'To hide it?' Dee wondered.

'Yeah, or worse,' Tim said. 'Maybe he's going to use it again? He could just create another universe, another reality – one where we don't even exist.'

'Or one where we're goldfish,' Dee said. 'Blind goldfish.'

'Yeah, or that.'

'Stopping him in blind-fish form would be virtually impossible,' Phil said.

'Then … I suppose this is our last chance.' Dee nodded.

Tim paced, thinking, planning – they had to get *out* of this cell and *in*to that basement, before Stephen did. He glanced up at the window. Even if they somehow got rid of the bars and broke the glass, it still wasn't big enough to crawl through. He turned back to the door. Double-locked, electronically *and* the old-fashioned way. It was possible Phil could remove the hinges with some metal-cutting equipment, but not without attracting a great deal of attention from the guards.

'We just can't do it alone,' Tim said with a wince, gesturing towards the door.

'Guys,' Dee said through the bars.

'Yeah.'

'Hmmm.'

'Ah!'

'How long have you three been on this wing?' Dee asked.

'Oh, longer than you could possibly imagine,' Hammer replied.

'Presumably you've thought about breaking out?' she said.

'Every day, but it can't be done,' Stabby Pete added. 'No one gets out of Hawk Peak.'

'What if we just needed to get out of *this wing*,' Dee said. 'What if we just needed to get to, say, that basement hatch? Could *that* be done?'

'I ... maybe, but it's a dead end,' Hammer said. 'One way in, one way out. Plus it's in the middle of the quad, which is a huge open space. Even *if* you made it that far, they'd catch you for sure.'

'That's absolutely fine – it only needs to be a one-way trip,' Dee said.

'Why are you asking? Is one of you small

enough to crawl through the bars?' Stabby Pete asked, sarcastically.

'Yep,' Dee said. 'One of us is a finger monkey.'

'Hello,' Phil said.

'What the hell is a finger monkey?'

'It's . . .' Tim said. 'It's like a monkey that's the size of a mouse.'

There was a pause.

'Cool,' Hammer said.

'That does sound brilliant,' Stabby Pete admitted.

'So, come on, run us through it,' Dee said.

'I ain't telling you nothin' until you kids explain what you have planned.' Hammer sounded stubborn.

'All right, listen,' Tim said. 'Couple of years back I met an inventor, Professor Eisenstone. He'd built this machine, this box . . .' He retold the whole story, right up to this very moment in time. Dee and Phil added bits of information every now and then.

'And I thought Screamy Joe was crazy,' Hammer said once Tim had finished. 'But you're my kind of crazy, so why the hell not. I'll tell ya how to get out to that hatch, but after that you're on your own. Firstly, do *not* tamper with your door. Any damage will initiate a full wing lockdown – sleeping gas will come out of the vents, alarms will sound, guards, drones, the works. You do *not* want that to happen. Instead, get that monkey of yours to break the control box near the end of the hall – that'll take care of the electronic autolocks. You'll need to use something powerful, ideally explosives.'

Phil's eyes lit up. 'That shan't be a problem.'

'The guard *will* come and investigate, so everything must happen quickly,' Hammer explained. 'You'll need to get his key *and* key card. You need two sets of hands to open the barrier door, to get to the window, you see. You *could* try and blast through it, but that'd also initiate lockdown. I suggest letting either me or Stabby Pete out and we can tackle the guard for you.'

'No way,' Tim whispered to Dee. 'Absolutely not. That's a no-no.' He really did not like the idea of coming into physical contact with these inmates. 'Phil can make a new key and key card.'

'There is no doubt that my imagination box is powerful,' the monkey whispered. 'But I am sorry to report it is also modest in size. Smaller, you will note, than a key card.'

'Well, hang on,' Dee whispered, before saying louder, 'Can I just ask what you did to get locked up in here?'

'Me?' Hammer said. 'Tax avoidance.'

'Why do they call you Hammer then?' Dee was frowning.

'That's my last name, Gerald Hammer.'

'And how about you Stabby Pete?' she asked.

'Streaking,' he said, with a sigh.

Tim and Dee's eyebrows lifted at the same time.

'As in, running naked on to, like, a football pitch?' she said.

'Ice hockey,' he explained. 'Twenty-six counts. Painful when they tackle you, but worth it.'

'O ... K ... Why are you called Stabby Pete then?' Dee wondered.

'Oh, I stabbed a guy too. But he's fine – we're actually dear friends now.'

'We can cross him off,' she whispered. 'Right, what about Screamy Joe?' Dee asked.

'Ah!'

'Best to leave Screamy Joe in his cell,' Hammer said.

They planned it all in perfectly timed detail – everyone had their roles and got themselves prepared. Before they started, Dee asked Hammer what the chances of success were. He laughed and sighed. 'You want the honest answer or the sugar-coated answer?' he said. 'Really, I'd be astonished if even *half* of this goes to plan. I reckon they'll catch you, or shoot you, within about, say, sixty seconds?'

'And the sugar-coated answer?' Tim said.

'I'm afraid that was the sugar-coated answer, kiddo.'

Tim and Dee looked at one another and she shrugged.

'Say something reassuring,' Tim whispered.

'Um, the Grey Guards use high-velocity rifles, so if we die it'll probably be instantaneous?' she said.

'Do you know what "reassuring" means? Aw, let's just do it.'

And so Phil scurried out through the door's narrow food hatch, climbed up to the fuse box and used his sharp teeth to chew through the alarm wire.

Then he used a marble-sized ball of plastic explosives (Philtex) to blast it to pieces. The lights flickered and the electronic autolocks whirred down. This, as expected, summoned the guard. The rest of the scheme happened out of Tim's sight, but he could hear the commotion well enough.

Spotting Phil, the guard chased him down the hall, presumably mistaking him for a mouse – Tim heard loud footsteps. The monkey darted into Hammer's cell. Once the guard stepped close to the bars, Hammer grabbed him and held him in place. Tim heard the guard yelling to be released, then giggling and screaming and wiggling as the monkey scurried into his pocket. A moment later, a door was clunking.

'No, stop, backup, I need backup!' the man shouted.

Hammer was then at their door, fiddling outside with the stolen key card. There was a beep. Then the real lock clacked and turned. It swung open, squeaking on its hinges. Tim was relieved to see the guard was unhurt and was now himself locked inside Hammer's cell.

'You're smaller than I imagined,' the inmate said as they stepped out into the hall.

'You're *bigger* than I imagined,' Tim replied, glancing up at the tall, heavyset man. Hammer had a vest and tattoos and a scary face. For a terrible moment Tim wondered if he had lied about his crimes and was actually planning to just kill and eat them. Or something along those lines.

Luckily, he was a really nice guy – a gentle giant. Dee snatched the keys from him, ran straight to the main door at the end of the hall, and snapped one off in the keyhole, blocking the lock. There were prison guards on the other side, shouting things at them and then into their radios – they seemed panicked to see inmates out of their cells.

She returned and Hammer guided them to the barrier door, which needed a card swipe and two locks turned in unison. On the other side was the window.

'Right,' he said, pointing outside. 'You see – there, in the middle of the courtyard – that's your hatch for the basement.'

It was further away than Tim had imagined.

The prison was huge and square in shape, with four large sections and an expanse of empty land in the middle. On the far side, Tim could see the five-storey building – the South Wing. Connected either side of that were the east and the west wings. There were hundreds of windows, all looking down into the courtyard area. It reminded him of school.

What struck Tim was how bare everything was – there were no trees, no benches, no colours out there. Just flat, empty concrete, enclosed by tall brick buildings. A few weeds had sprouted through cracks, but besides that it looked almost abandoned.

A second ball of explosives turned a chunk of concrete wall to dust, removing bolts around the now cracked glass.

Grunting, Hammer barged the damaged window frame with his shoulder, shattering the rest and bending the metal lattice. He then put a foot on the wall and, with bulging veins and clenched teeth, pried it open, only just wide enough for Tim and Dee.

The guards at the end of the hall were nearly through the door now as Hammer held his thick fingers together between his knees, giving both Tim and Dee a lift through. It seemed effortless, not because they were light but because he was strong.

'Thanks, Mr Hammer,' Tim said, landing outside in the colder air.

They turned to run, but Hammer said, 'Wait. Tim, you can change everything with this machine?'

'Yeah, that's right.'

'Could you change my life?' Hammer seemed suddenly small, like a child younger than Tim asking for a treat.

'Well, maybe,' Tim said. 'What is it you want?'

'I just ... I just want to be happy,' Hammer whispered.

An alarm – a constant ringing, like a school bell left on – began to play above.

The guards were through the door and, with a frantic rush, were tackling Hammer to the ground, clicking cuffs around his wrists and yelling.

Ignoring their orders – which included, 'Freeze', 'Stop' and every variation on that theme – Tim and Dee ran, Hammer's words echoing in his mind. They scaled a fence and were then on the wide-open expanse of concrete. Right in the centre, Tim could just about see the small metal door imbedded in the ground.

'Come on,' he said. 'There it is.'

However, they had only taken about three paces when a spotlight dazzled his vision – stinging white light, brighter than the sun. It was attached, Tim noticed, to a helicopter, which rumbled above and then swooped quickly into the middle of the courtyard. Dust swirled and curled beneath its blades as it touched down. Two watchtowers on the far side came alive – another pair of searchlights shone down on them. Then two more from behind. They were now lit like footballers in a stadium – four shadows splitting at their feet like points on a compass.

Shielding his face, Tim could see far up ahead that armed Grey Guards were getting into formation. They were all wearing full combat gear, complete with dark helmets, boots, bulletproof vests – the works. There were at least fifty of them, some crouching behind riot shields, others lying prone on the floor, cocking rifles and reporting on radios. More were appearing at the windows, a few were running into position on the rooftop. Little red lasers – dots of death – arrived on Tim and Dee.

'They sure are taking this seriously,' she said, looking down at her chest.

Tim stood there, dancing drops of gentle rain still falling around him like glowing dust, and, despite all the noise and chaos, he could still hear his own pulse throbbing inside his head. Would they *actually* shoot them if they made a run for that hatch, Tim wondered.

'Phil, where's your imagination box?' Tim whispered.

'Oh, dirty fiddlesticks,' the monkey said. 'I left it in the cell. Everything was so rushed.'

'Shame, you could have made a hat.'

'Salt my open wounds.'

And then a megaphone echoed from the helicopter. 'Don't move a muscle.'

Tim recognised his voice straight away.

Stephen Crowfield strode out from behind the spotlight, his long leather jacket waving in the wind, flapping near his feet. He stepped towards the hatch and, without thinking, Tim started walking forwards too. He couldn't let Stephen get there first. But the moment he moved, all the red dots and spotlights centred on him.

'I said *don't* move.' Stephen was holding the megaphone to his mouth as he walked.

Helpless, they could only watch as he opened the hatch and disappeared inside the ground. He stepped out carrying a large metal container – the imagination station presumably enclosed within. Like a cannonball in his chest, Tim's heart ached in defeat. His fists were clenched at his sides. They had come *so close*.

'Put your hands above your head,' another amplified voice said from behind the lights.

'He's got it,' Tim said, panicked and sweating, lifting his arms a little. They were shaking. Stephen was walking calmly back towards his helicopter. 'We ... we have to ...' But he couldn't find the words.

Sometimes he tried to make himself think like Dee, with pure, cold logic. The facts were: if he moved, his life would probably end. But then if he *didn't* move, his life would probably end too.

'Timothy, I have an idea,' Phil said from his shirt pocket.

'Is it get shot and then die?' Dee said out of the side of her mouth. 'Cos I think that's pretty doable.'

'No, it is better than that.'

'I'm all ears,' Tim said, staring into the distance, past the lights, at all those gun barrels.

'It is going to hurt,' Phil said. 'A lot.'

'What is?'

The monkey scurried up Tim's chest and on to his shoulder. 'The chip in your neck,' Phil whispered.

The chip in my neck, Tim thought to himself, moving it around under his skin with his index finger. The small device that was stopping him from instantly projecting whatever he could imagine into the real world. The tiny piece of technology that was keeping sabre-toothed tigers, fire and who knows what else caged up in his mind.

'We said: hands above your head!' Stephen's voice echoed again, now with anger, as he turned round and faced them.

The monkey stroked the short pink scar on Tim's

neck. 'Sharp teeth,' Phil whispered. 'I will, of course, require your consent.'

Tensing his jaw, Tim nodded. 'Do it.'

A moment of spectacular pain – it felt like a pair of pliers pinching his skin. But, a second later, in what seemed slow motion, Tim saw Phil spit something out. He watched the chip glisten and spin and fall in front of him. Still glossed slightly red with his blood, it clattered to the concrete at his feet. His hearing was whirring, everything seemed dizzy, out of focus. Pressing his sleeve into his fresh wound he stepped forwards and crushed the piece of metal under his shoe.

This was apparently enough movement – or maybe Stephen had anticipated the potential danger. Either way, he lifted his megaphone and turned to his men.

'Open fire,' he said.

And, without a moment's hesitation, they did.

Chapter 21

Across Hawk Peak Prison's large courtyard, behind the glare of searchlights, little orange stars were appearing and disappearing. Hundreds of gun muzzles flashing in the dark – it really was quite a sight, Tim thought, calmly. Phil was hidden back in Tim's top pocket and Dee had covered her head, turned and curled downwards towards the ground. This was a fairly reasonable way to react to incoming gunfire, after all.

It was pretty outrageous, actually, Tim thought now – his ears still whirring from the pain of Phil's bite. Sure, they probably knew him as the kid who could conjure a cobra with the power of his mind and he was, of course, a security-level-five most-wanted suspect, whatever that meant. But shooting unarmed children? That sounded far worse than all the things he'd done combined.

All these thoughts played out in less time than it takes to blink. And then ...

His hearing came back – an insane roar of gunshots and ricochets and carnage as bullets zipped and pinged and sparked off the half dome of glass that had appeared. Tim hadn't consciously imagined that a bulletproof shield would materialise between them and the firing squad – it had just kind of happened. In the same way you automatically blink when something approaches your face, Tim's subconscious was just taking care of business.

The gunfire stopped for a moment and the wide sheet of thick glass – frosted and cracked – tilted and fell heavily on the ground, exposing them again.

Dee lowered her arms from her face, looking up to Tim and then to the guards. She was glaring – maybe in shock, maybe excitement. He had previously explained that he had this ability – telling her how unstable and dangerous it was, hence the chip – but he supposed actually seeing it in action was still quite incredible for her.

Up ahead, Stephen and the Grey Guards were waiting – waiting for something else to happen, waiting for an explanation, Tim couldn't be sure. But quiet and waiting they remained.

The alarm bell clicked off now and the parked helicopter's blades were still. No one spoke. No one moved.

There was silence . . .

One thing Tim had noticed about Hawk Peak Prison was that it was quite grey. Sparse. No colour. No music. No soul.

'This place needs some . . . imagination,' Tim said, helping Dee to her feet.

He turned to face the guards, bowed his head and lifted his hands as though he was surrendering. But, instead, he took a slow breath in and, as he exhaled, pushed his palms forwards and set his mind free. A wide and tall invisible wall of air opened up, like a portal to some other dimension, and out came everything Tim could imagine.

It was a stampede, a charging army, everything appearing all at once just in front of them, spread evenly across the entire width of the courtyard and running forwards, towards the guards. There were giant rhinos, bear-sharks scrambling over each other, a T. rex emerging and lowering its head for an angry war cry. A marching band to the left, dressed smartly in red-and-white blazers, thumping drums and cymbals and trumpets, their music louder than gunfire as they marched confidently forwards in formation.

A pair of long, dark green dragons spiralled out into existence, flying up and curving over themselves above, like giant eels in a tank, thick flares of fire criss-crossing as heavy wings sent harsh winds down on to the guards below. Creatures beyond description, monsters of every kind, stomped and barged and yelled. A giant, a Cyclops, some kind of awful badger thing threw a car. Some terrifying, others simply ridiculous. Parts of the courtyard erupting now in a fountain of liquid chocolate or a spew of lava or a torrent of water or a frenzy of frogs. One corner seemed dedicated to jam, another to the jungle.

Colours exploded above, reds and yellows and blues, neon pinks and fluorescent greens, powdered paint and fireworks lighting up and spreading a vibrant fog. Within these clouds, forks of lightning fired overhead like synapses in a brain.

There were paper lanterns and other inanimate objects too, chairs and tables rolling amid the carnage, and things Tim had seen or idly thought about years ago – distant memories finding form. Strange pieces of metal and wood – raw materials and odd bits of matter appearing for reasons Tim would never understand. Some objects simply coming into existence in mid-air then falling to the ground. He saw a sack of carrots tumble in the middle of a horde of what looked like rabbits with wheels – an odd hybrid of a toy he had once seen. Behind that a full-sized galleon smashed down and rolled over, sliding into the concrete, broken wood, slack sails and ropes, pirates leaping and swinging into action.

For Tim, it felt as though all his childhood sketchpads were coming alive, as though they were being held open and shaken.

Most of all, the whole experience was liberating, a huge relief. Before he had been on his toes, worried about creating the wrong thing, worried about his imagination getting out of hand. But now he was letting it roam free off the leash. And the results looked and felt equally brilliant. There it all went, doing battle with Stephen's army of armed clones.

Things were still materialising – fairy lights running the hundreds of metres around the prison, fairground banners and confetti – as Tim scanned across, searching amid the insanity. There. He spotted Stephen, clutching the metal imagination station to his chest, darting, scared, through a door and inside the East Wing.

'Come on,' Tim said, stepping back towards the window they'd come through, pulling Dee by her hand.

Getting around was easier now. When Tim came to a locked door or, in this instance, a brick wall, he just raised a hand and imagined it replaced by thin air. And, with a fizzle and crumble of dust, the wall simply opened up. They entered the prison together, leaving the medley outside. With a casual wave, Tim made the wall reappear behind them, without even looking.

'Tim, wait,' Dee said. 'This is … this is crazy.' The chaos outside was still loud – there was music, shouting and even the odd explosion and distant clatter of panicked gunfire.

'Did I spy a dinosaur in amongst all that?' Phil added.

'Probably a few.' Tim nodded.

'All those Grey Guards, will they be OK?' Dee asked.

'If they've got any sense, they'll run away,' Tim said. 'Look, Stephen went into the East Wing. We've still got to get the imagination station, all right? Quickly too. This ability of mine is not entirely a good thing.'

'Why didn't he just use it in the basement?'

'I dunno. I guess he has to charge it up? And he'll need somewhere quiet to concentrate. All I know is that while we're *here*, alive and walking around, there is still a chance.'

'All right,' Dee said. 'This way.' She pointed to a sign to the East Wing above them.

They ran down the corridors, past inmates locked in their cells – all of whom were at their windows which were glowing and flashing like television screens. Everywhere smelled faintly of candyfloss, freshly cooked doughnuts and clean, salty air. Tim had thought briefly of the seaside.

'Smells lovely,' Dee said.

Arriving in the East Wing of the prison, they crossed a few abandoned security checkpoints – all the staff were outside and most of *these* cells were empty. Then, with a clunk, all the lights went out, the prison's backup power whirring on a second later, lighting everything faintly blue. It was gloomy and cold in here, the exact opposite to outside.

Tim managed to melt one locked door by imagining heat – they stepped carefully over a glowing glob of white-hot metal. Another locked door he turned to jelly, which they simply pushed down. It was easier to create strange things, with specific textures and smells, he found. If his mind wandered, his abilities faded. He was betting that Stephen couldn't move around the prison as quickly as them, and was hoping he was hiding *somewhere* in this wing. All they had to do was find him.

'So, Timothy, did you create that eclectic mix of creatures outside to be kind to us?' Phil asked, licking some lemon door-jelly from his fingers.

'Yeah, that's a good point,' Dee said, jogging along. 'I'm sure some of that madness will have made it inside.'

'I . . . no, not really,' Tim said. 'I didn't really think about any of them, I just let it all out.'

'Tell you what you should create: a tracking device,' Dee added. 'Or . . . or a sniffer dog—'

There was a noise up ahead. Tim stopped and grabbed Dee by the shoulder. Something round the corner was snuffling and breathing.

'What is that?' Dee asked.

A long shadow at first, then the sound of hooves clip-clopping on the tiled floor. At the end of the hall a perfectly white horse emerged. It brayed and stood noble and proud. A tail flicked, its thick muscles twitched, velvety hair glistening in the half-light. It was a surreal thing to see in a narrow prison corridor.

'Whoa,' Dee said, sighing in relief. 'A horse. Something nice for once.'

Then Tim noticed a long horn in the centre of the animal's head.

'That is no horse,' Phil said. 'That is a unicorn.'

'Hang on.' Tim couldn't even remember creating the creature, but something about the way it stood filled him with fear.

'It's beautiful,' Dee added.

However, when the animal turned and spotted them, it completely changed. It lowered its head, rolled back its lips and hissed. Tim saw that it had fangs and wild red eyes.

'Ah,' Phil said. 'I note with interest that it appears to be quite the predator.' There was a smug, I-told-you-so tone.

'This doesn't prove anything,' Tim whispered, stepping backwards slowly. 'You just planted the idea in my head.'

With a deafening screech, the unicorn broke into a crazed gallop, hurtling towards them.

'What?' Dee stood stunned.

'Timothy, quickly, create a wall or a trap or something,' Phil yelled.

'All right,' Tim said as the creature charged, its mad scream rising.

He concentrated hard but, instead of a solution, he created more problems. *Another* unicorn appeared at the end of the corridor, behind the first one.

'Gosh, what peril,' Phil said.

'I can't,' Tim yelled. 'I can't get my thoughts straight. No, no, no.' He held up his hands and scrunched his face.

Just before it arrived, Dee shoved Tim against the wall and dived to the floor on the other side of the corridor. The heavy beast swung its horn – a razor-pointed sting – which cut through the air, just missing Tim's face. It scrambled, slipping clumsily on the tiles and sliding on its side into a metal detector, sending a swivel chair spinning as it kicked out with strong legs.

'Obviously run,' Dee said as the unicorn rose quickly and began to chase them again.

The second one had also joined in and, now, another one too. Running desperately down the nearby prison corridor, Tim looked over his shoulder to see all of them in pursuit. Two white ones and a larger, scarier, black one.

'Ah, there's three of them,' Dee shouted as they turned a corner, hooves and snapping jaws slamming against the wall behind.

'I think they hunt in packs,' Phil yelled.

'Shut up, Phil,' Tim said.

'The big one is the alpha,' the monkey added. 'Just like velociraptors.'

They arrived in a large cafeteria area and pushed quickly through doors into a quiet kitchen.

Tim had almost forgotten about the chaos outside. It was only when he looked through the window and saw two huge animals, which he could only describe as bat-dolphins with knives for feet, did he wish he'd been less creative with his artwork. So much weird stuff in his brain, he thought.

But at least most of that was out there. In *here* they had to contend with a pack of bloodthirsty unicorns, which were now sniffing the air and stalking between the long dining tables in the cafeteria next door. Tim shoved a chair under the door handle and they crouched.

Dee held a finger to her lips. The sound of hooves on the hard floor was terrifying, but thankfully it was getting quieter and quieter.

'I suspect,' Phil whispered, 'that a unicorn's predisposition to ultraviolence is territorial. We must give them space.'

After a while Tim turned his head and couldn't hear them any more.

'OK, I think they've lost us,' he whispered, gently opening the door an inch to peep. The coast looked clear. He turned back to Dee. 'Let's be quick and—'

A head smashed inside, writhing and screeching. Tim shouted a swear word as he fell away, knocked to the floor. The creature was stuck there, the door lodged in place with the chair.

Tim bounced back to his feet and they circled through the other kitchen door into the cafeteria. One of the remaining unicorns struck, but Dee kicked over a table – it slammed its horn through the wood, leaving it stuck in place over its eyes. Panicked, it shook its head and ran straight into a wall, knocking itself clean out.

Two down, one to go.

Tim and Dee left the cafeteria and ran the length of two long corridors and round another corner, arriving at the foot of a wide stairwell. They went straight up to the second floor and peered down over the bannister, catching their breath and checking the third and final animal – the alpha – had given up the chase. However, it appeared below them, searching the air for a scent like a hunting dog.

'We can relax,' Dee said. 'I'm ninety per cent sure horses can't go upstairs, so I'm guessing unicorns can't either.'

Its neck jerked up and its eyes locked on them. 'Oh yes we can,' it said in a horribly gurgled, demonic voice.

'What the … It can talk? That makes them so much worse,' Dee said. 'Tim, what the hell is wrong with you?'

'Blame Phil.'

'Who you also created?'

'She's got you there, old sonny chap.'

The unicorn was coming up the stairs now, mumbling in its hissing, monstrous voice. 'Imma eat you, gonna munch-munch your face. *Yum, yum, yum-yum-yum,*' with each clumsy step.

'For God's sake,' Dee said.

Again, they ran – only to find themselves at a dead end. They turned to see the awful thing standing right there, just a couple of metres away. It was by a large window, lit strangely blue in the dawn light. Tim supposed much of the chaos outside had eased by this point as it was quieter now.

'I can't die like this,' Dee said, pressing against the wall. 'It's too weird.'

The unicorn slunk low, growling and exposing its dripping fangs. With a final snarl, it pounced, but—

A vast mass of scaled flesh and teeth smashed through the window by its side, crumbling bricks with ease. In a blink, the unicorn was slammed into the opposite wall, squeezed between huge dragon jaws. And, almost as quick as it arrived, the giant head pulled out and disappeared through a gaping hole in the side of the prison, a few pieces of concrete and rubble falling into the corridor. A wire sparked in the cold air, illuminating the blood and glitter left behind.

'Well, I say,' Phil whispered.

They continued through the dark prison and, realising Stephen could have hidden anywhere, Tim calmed himself down and did what Dee suggested, creating a sniffer dog – a Labrador. It had polka dots and a pink tail, for which he could only apologise. But it did its job well. It took off running quickly, leading them further upstairs and on to the roof.

The dog – named Barry in honour of Barry – looked up at a tall guard tower on the corner of the prison building and barked twice.

Sure enough, in the window, Tim could see a figure looking down at all the commotion in the courtyard. A lot of the creatures were fighting each other now – the marching band still dutifully providing the soundtrack. There was an insane amount of mess too. The courtyard looked like a giant, cluttered toy box – just too much random activity to even begin to explain. Tim couldn't tell where one creation began and the next ended.

One thing he did spot though, lurching in the jungle area, was a red monster. It was an exact copy of the beast Clarice Crowfield had accidently created with her imagination box – the image of it obviously still clear in Tim's mind.

'Really is strange all that,' Dee whispered, looking over the railing.

They told Barry he was a good boy and then used the ladder to scale the tower. Dee helped Tim to his feet on the metal balcony. Crouching, they snuck round to the door and gently eased it open.

On the table, in the middle of the small room, sat the imagination station, charging up from a mains socket. Tim had previously thought this need for power was a design flaw, but now he was grateful – these extra few minutes before it could be used had made all the difference.

It was exactly like the drawing Tim had seen that day in Rick Harris's office at TRAD. A flat, dark grey metal box with a tall container perched on top. Suspended in translucent liquid, barely visible through the tinted viewing window, was the replica of Tim's brain. It stood to attention, perfectly still, held in place by the spine of wires leading into the back of it. And the reader, attached to the base by coiled cables, like a heavy tail, was at the side of the machine. Just seeing it felt like a victory in itself.

They crept inside a little further but, when they were just a metre or so away from it, Stephen spotted them. He dived across the room and grabbed the device under his arm – it looked heavy and cumbersome, but he still moved fast. Without a word, he stumbled desperately towards the opposite door. However, Tim stood upright, waved a hand and the door was instantly a wall. Stephen slammed against the new bricks, confused. Tim was calmer now – seeing the imagination station, he knew he was back in the driving seat. Again, Stephen scrambled for another exit but was stopped when Tim sealed that one too.

'Stephen,' Tim whispered. 'Hand it over.'

Hugging the contraption to his chest, Stephen shook his head, stepping backwards. 'No.'

Dee sighed. 'You're not in a strong position, buddy,'

she said. 'Tim could turn your blood to boiling custard just by thinking it. That'd be Deadville for you. Corpse Avenue.'

Tim put his hand on his forehead and winced, making sure that didn't accidently happen. 'No, Dee, don't say that.'

'You can't have it. I . . . I haven't had enough time,' Stephen said. And then his eyes flashed with an idea, a sudden realisation. 'This is how things are, *this* is how they have to stay.'

With that Tim watched, glaring and shaking his head, as Stephen pulled a handgun from his inside jacket pocket. For a moment Tim thought he might shoot him, or Dee, or perhaps even himself. But, instead, he placed the barrel of the pistol against the machine's glass, pointing at the human brain enclosed within.

'I'm sorry,' he said. He closed his eyes and squeezed the trigger.

Chapter 22

Once again, Tim's mind acted in reflex, driven by anger and fear and shock. However, this time, he had no real idea what was happening.

He knew, after Stephen pulled that trigger – that if a bullet drove its way through the imagination station, through that brain – they may well be stuck in this reality forever. So, without thinking, Tim scrunched his face up, grasped his head and whispered, 'No.'

The air around them seemed to thicken and tingle with static as Stephen watched the pistol leave his grip, floating up into the middle of the room, Tim guiding it with an invisible force he didn't understand. It was suspended there, hovering, waiting, aiming now at the ceiling. There was a brief silence and then, when Tim exhaled, the gun went off and a shockwave blasted out from him, shattering glass and bricks and furniture.

The sudden release triggered an earthquake – the ground lurched violently left and right and everyone in the watchtower was slammed on to the floor, pressed there by another unexplained force. Tim realised that it was, in fact, G-force that squeezed him, Dee and Stephen on the rumbling floor.

For reasons his conscious mind couldn't fully grasp, he made a tall brick tower appear beneath them. A large, skyscraper-sized column that tore the entire room from its metal frame legs and drove it – and everything inside – up into the air.

Lying on the ground, dazed, Tim's mind took yet more precautions. He looked up and the ceiling disappeared, replaced instantly with thin air. What remained of the walls faded away too. The scattered furniture went next, then the gun, Tim clearing away everything besides himself, Phil, Dee, Stephen and the imagination station.

Less than ten seconds after Stephen had pulled out the pistol, they were all lying on top of a wide, empty platform, with nothing but clear sky around them. Tim crawled carefully to the edge and, still surprised by where he found himself, placed his fingers over the new bricks to look straight down.

'Uhh,' he said, realising how high they were.

To his right, the sun was just behind the horizon, sending warm orange and morning purple on to the underside of hazy clouds. Tim looked over and out to sea, noticing the rising light and the curve of the earth. Trapped in the prison, he had forgotten that Hawk Peak was so close to the ocean. The air was fresh up here and the water looked as though it might just go on forever. He gazed along the cliffs of the coast, which ran off in a wiggly line. Three curious crows were circling above and a faint breeze was whistling.

Beneath he could see the base of the tower, bricks spreading out organically like the roots of a great tree. He could also see the prison, just a small square now, with strange colours and odd things strewn about the middle. Luckily the majority of Tim's creations were contained within the four large wings of the building.

However, one of the dinosaurs was marching idly across a nearby wheat field and there was some commotion in the car park – a couple of fires and some more police arriving. What must they think of this daunting new tower growing out of the corner of the prison?

'What the hell is going on?' Stephen asked, standing now.

Tim shuffled away from the edge, stood and walked across to the imagination station.

'I should ask you the same,' he said, crouching to check the machine was still intact. A few scratches, but no serious damage. Tim eyed Stephen warily and said, 'Sit down.'

'Where?' Stephen asked, looking at the empty floor.

'There.' Tim pointed as a chair appeared. He made one for him and Dee too.

Stephen sat. It was obvious he had given up. Even someone who'd tasted such power knew when they were defeated.

There was still so much about this universe that confused Tim. 'Why? Why did you do it?' he asked, not angrily, but out of pure curiosity.

Stephen stared across the horizon. 'She ... my mother, she came back.'

'Yeah,' Tim said. 'I know. I know the man who repaired the teleporter – he made this thing too.' He groaned as he heaved the imagination station up on to a new table. It was heavier than he thought it would be.

Squirming, Stephen seemed almost ashamed.

'I don't understand though,' Tim added, turning back to him. 'Why would you help her again?'

Stephen struggled to find the right words. 'After what happened, at Crowfield House,' he finally said, looking heartbroken at the memory. 'I couldn't sleep. I could hardly eat. I just felt so ... so guilty.'

'Well, I'm no psychiatrist,' Dee said, 'but teleporting your own mum into oblivion is not the kind of thing you just forget.'

'She was ... awful to me,' Stephen said. 'And, yes, I hated her for it. But ... but she was still my mother – she still brought me into this world. When I heard she was alive, I was ... I was relieved.'

'So you broke into TRAD, what, to make it

up to her?' Tim said. 'Sorry about the attempted murder, here's a universe where all your dreams have come true?'

'Kind of, yeah. We hoped to teleport into the Diamond Building, but Fredric was too stubborn, too *scared* of the technology.' Stephen seemed so exhausted that he was happy to just tell them everything. 'Instead, a bit of petrol and I slipped in disguised as a firefighter, using a key card mother stole from the upper floors to get to the restricted areas. Nothing changes the state of things quite like fire.'

This was not the first time the Crowfields had used fire to get their way, Tim reflected. However, this time, it wasn't Clarice who got her hands dirty. 'But then you used it, the imagination station – *you* used it yourself,' Tim said.

'I was meant to hand the device over to her,' Stephen went on. 'But once I understood it, I knew I could make a better world than she could. You know what she was like. Can you *imagine* what sort of terrible place she would want to create? So I put the reader on and ... honestly, I wasn't expecting it to actually work … but, then …' He looked up at the sky, still amazed.

'Why pick on *me* though?' Tim asked. 'I woke up in Glassbridge Orphanage, alone. My family, my friends, no one knew who I was.'

This was by far the most bewildering part for Tim.

'I'm sorry, I really am,' Stephen said. 'But I did it for your own good. What if there was still some part of her that remembered? Still wanted revenge for Crowfield House? I hid you away to keep you safe.'

'But … but you left me able to remember everything?' Tim said. 'Why? Why not just erase my memories? Did you *honestly* think I would just accept it all? Were you punishing me?'

'No … no. It wasn't meant to happen that way,' Stephen said. 'It wasn't how I imagined it. But it's—'

'It's what?' Tim snapped.

Stephen took in a long breath. 'Rick wrote about how the machine works, how the imagination station does what it does.' He looked towards the ocean. 'There are an infinite number of universes,' he said. 'Which means every possible scenario, every conceivable arrangement of atomic matter, exists. Somewhere out there in the endless fabric of space and time, it's all happening. Like a radio, the machine simply tunes in to one of these realities and your imagination dictates the frequency, it dictates the *station*.'

Tim nodded, frowning – it was a simple explanation for an extremely complex thing. An infinite number of universes, he thought to himself. This was just one of them.

'And it's all thanks to the power of the human mind,' Stephen added. 'Your mind, Tim. The brain inside the jar. *That* is why you remember everything – that is the one thing I didn't see coming, the one glitch in this system. I picked this world, but *you* made it . . .'

Tim looked through the glass of the imagination station. It was a difficult thing to comprehend.

'So, Timothy is still the architect of everything,' Phil said. 'You have simply hijacked his imagination.'

'Wait, hang on,' Dee said, thinking aloud. 'The brain Tim created, the one in that machine, it created all of this. So he is a creation, of his own creation.'

'It's like a photo of a photo,' Stephen added. 'You can't change the original. I tried to delete your memories, but your brain made a faithful copy of you – I suppose only the "master mind" would have that power. Either way, that's why you didn't fit into your new life. I tried to make it good, I gave you a loyal friend – loyal enough to lie to the police for you – and a safe place to live. You *should* have been happy.'

In the weirdest possible way, that was almost a kind thing, Tim thought. Maybe Stephen wasn't all *that* bad – and yet . . .

'What about killing Fredric?' Dee asked 'What about framing us?'

'What else could I have done?' Stephen said. 'When you made contact with him, I knew something was wrong. Those paths should not have crossed. I realised that you remembered – that you knew the truth. Luckily, I had positioned myself well to handle something like that. My mother *thinks* she is an ultimate ruler, but I command the Grey Guards, *I* have the real power here. Me, you and Fredric were the only people on this earth who knew about the imagination station. It was a case of two birds with one stone. He's gone, and you're wanted for his murder.'

'And Granddad?' Dee asked. 'Have you murdered him too?'

'Don't worry. He's safe, somewhere, locked up in another prison I expect. I wouldn't hurt someone without a good reason.'

'So, then, for what reason did you keep Fredric around, with his memories?' Phil asked, sitting now on the edge of the table. 'You really risked it all for a petty punishment?'

There was half a smirk on Stephen's face. 'I told him that he would regret not helping me.'

'But then you killed him anyway,' Dee said. 'That is messed up.'

Stephen rolled his eyes – and Tim saw just how much he looked like his mother. He actually looked skinnier, paler and, well, somehow uglier than Tim remembered. He seemed weak. Was this how he saw himself?

'Oh, come on. Fredric was nothing,' Stephen said.

'Have you forgotten what *he* did? He was a murderer – are you really sad he's dead?'

Tim wasn't necessarily *sad* about Fredric, but he *was* surprised to hear how cold Stephen was being. It wasn't hard to understand why he was such a messed-up guy, what with his upbringing, but Tim had never realised just how much of Clarice there was in him.

'What?' Stephen said, noticing Tim's reaction. 'So I arranged to have someone murdered? Sue me.'

Phil shook his head. 'Oh, Clarice can indeed create monsters.'

That was it, Tim realised. That was why Stephen had made himself this way, made himself into a mean, spiteful person. The kind of man who would murder someone without remorse. The kind of man who would order armed guards to shoot unarmed children.

'You've become everything your mother said you were,' Tim said. 'If someone tells you that you're no good, eventually you'll start believing it. Eventually, it'll become true.'

'Judge me all you want. You don't know what it's like.' Stephen looked close to tears. 'To grow up and feel alone.'

'I know exactly what that's like,' Tim said.

'But I got nothing but *hate* from the person who is meant to love me the most,' Stephen whispered.

'Arson, murder, interdimensional shifts in reality?' Phil added, stroking his chin. 'All for something as simple as affection from your mother. You are quite the psychological case study, young Stephen Crowfield.'

'And what about you, Tim?' Stephen said, composing himself. He gestured over the edge of the bricks, to the prison below. 'What makes you special? You're going to put that reader on your head and use the imagination station? You've carved a path of destruction through my world, so what makes you think *you* can create a better one?'

'I ...' Tim paused. He couldn't really answer that question. The task seemed too daunting.

'You have not addressed your worst crime of all,' Phil said. 'Why would you desire a universe without chocolate?'

Sighing, Stephen let out a short laugh. 'I'm lactose intolerant, so I guess that's where that came from.' He shrugged.

'You have no soul,' the monkey said.

Tim took a deep breath. He'd heard enough. 'Goodbye, Stephen,' he said.

A lift had appeared at the edge of the tower behind him, and Tim nodded at it.

Patting his legs and sighing again, Stephen stood from the chair and strolled slowly to the new elevator. The doors slid open and he glanced around the interior, before stepping inside. He turned back and faced them, blinking in the golden sunrise.

'Well, see you on the other side,' he said with a casual salute.

'Let's hope not,' Tim replied.

The doors slid closed, the lift descended. And, just like that, Stephen Crowfield was gone.

Chapter 23

Now alone on the tower, high above all the guards and creatures and colours below, Tim and Dee sat at the table. Tim pulled the imagination station towards him. All this potential, he thought, contained in such a small thing. And then Stephen's words echoed in his ears – the power of the human mind. Tim always felt uneasy when he thought about his own brain, and here it was, a perfect replica suspended in liquid, running this machine. Everything he had ever seen or done, the memories that made him who he was, every single thought and emotion – it was all ultimately contained within the dark, confined space inside his skull. All just the consequence of a few electrical signals shooting around a squidgy lump of wet stuff. This thought made him feel nervous and small.

'A brain,' he whispered. 'A mind. A universe.'

'So, yeah, to recap: new reality,' Dee said. 'I would like to be rich – not crazy rich, just *quite rich*. Enough cash to own a boat, but not so much that I forget to value it, you know? Also can I be a smidge taller. Again, don't go crazy – I want to look normal . . . and, and . . .'

She carried on listing her demands, counting them on her fingers, all the things she wants from life. Or, Tim thought, all the things she *thinks* she wants. He thought then of what Hammer said at the window. All *he* wanted was to be happy. But, beyond that, he couldn't be specific.

'You were right,' Tim whispered. 'Stephen was right. I don't know how to make a better universe.'

'Timothy,' Phil said, sitting perched on the edge of the table just in front of the imagination station, 'I am afraid to say, I think the window in which we could feasibly do nothing has long since passed.'

'Yeah, we're still wanted felons here,' Dee said.

'And Granddad is still locked up somewhere. Not to mention all those things down there.'

They were right. Tim knew he had to do *something*. Staying in this reality was not an option – especially with his rampant powers of imagination back off the leash. 'I … I could create my idea of a perfect life,' he said. 'If I knew what it was.'

'There must be things you want?' Dee said.

'I want …'

What *did* Tim want? He wanted things back to how they were – he wanted a family, a mother. Someone who would be there, someone who would ask how he was and care about the answer, someone who would give him advice on anything in the whole wide world. Someone like Elisa. He wanted that garden he'd imagined at the new hotel, a rose arch and fairy lights in the bushes. Short grass and long, simple evenings spent in a tree house. The smell of summer. He wanted to feel safe.

He thought again of Elisa, of what she said to him the night before everything changed.

'Elisa can't have babies,' Tim said, thinking aloud.

'O . . . K?' Dee said.

'She told me she was sad when she first found out. Like, really sad,' Tim said. 'Not being able to create life . . . she said it made her cry.'

'I have long pondered the meaning of life,' Phil added. 'It seems propagating your respective species is the only answer that comes close to being objectively right. Even microbes, nay *even plants*, sign up to that.'

'Yeah, getting upset about not being able to have children makes sense,' Dee said. 'I saw a documentary on it once. People love having kids. What's your point?'

'The point is that, in the end, she *wasn't* upset,' Tim explained. 'She said it was a good thing, really. It meant she got to adopt me, and that made her happy.'

Dee sat silently for a moment, nodding.

'I completely understand what she meant,' Tim said. 'All I wanted growing up was a normal family life. I didn't really know it, but I think that's what I wanted. I was always lonely at Glassbridge Orphanage. And the dream, what I hoped would happen – it didn't have a busy hotel for my home, a stress-ball maniac like Elisa as a mum, a busy dad who's rarely there like Chris. But that's exactly what I want now.'

'The unmatched beauty of imperfection,' Phil added, stroking his oddly striped tail.

'Maybe paradise is impossible,' Tim said, staring now into the distance. He could see for miles across the ocean, the surface a pattern of glinting white shards in the sun. 'If I don't even know what's best for me, how the hell can I decide what's best for other people?'

'So, what's in store?' Dee asked. 'What are you actually going to think about when you use the imagination station?'

Before he was arrested, Professor Eisenstone had actually told Tim what needed to happen. At the time, Tim didn't really understand. But now it was as clear as this very morning.

'I know what to do,' he said. 'I am going to create a universe where none of this has happened. A world where I never even discover the imagination box, a reality where I never go into Eisenstone's room that day and accidently imagine a sausage into existence.'

'Undo it all.' Dee echoed her grandfather's words.

'I'll ... I'll make it ... I'll make everything exactly as it was, but with *one* difference,' Tim said. 'I'll still sneak into the function room to steal a cake, I'll still see the professor. But that day, I went in his room because the door didn't shut properly. So, I'll make it so room nineteen's door *does* close. Everything the same, but with a single, tiny tweak, one that has the maximum impact.'

'But what about Clarice? What about everything that happened?' Dee asked.

'They kidnapped Eisenstone because we'd made the box work,' Tim said, speaking quickly. 'Without it working they'd have given up. They were waiting for proof. Everything happened because of that precise moment. It all traces back to that day.'

It seemed so obvious now, Tim thought. It really was the only fair way. If Eisenstone was willing to give up his greatest scientific success, then Tim could too.

'The professor said this machine shouldn't exist,' he added.

Phil looked over his shoulder at the imagination station, and nodded.

'It means you'll be back to square one with Elisa,' Dee said. 'She'll be all stressed again.'

'We'll get there,' Tim said.

'And me and you?' Dee was frowning. 'We'll never meet. We'll never become friends.'

It was worse than that, Tim realised, feeling a real chill in the air.

'No imagination box, no talking finger monkey,' Phil whispered.

A gloom descended over them, a rain cloud quickly forming above, a flat covering of grey. It happened so quickly that it was obviously the work of Tim's mind, his emotions escaping into the real world. He thought it was somehow silly, but he couldn't help it.

Phil wiggled his tiny feet, putting on a brave face. 'In summary, I concur,' he said. 'It is the only option. You are right about that.'

'I just …' Tim whispered. 'Maybe … maybe you could still exist, maybe …'

The monkey shook his head. 'You cannot play

God. Any decision you make might be wrong, the consequences unknowable. It is a one-way street, irreversible, no way back. So it must be as close to the natural order of things as possible. You must not remember any of it – only *you* can make that happen.' He held his small hand out and Tim put his index finger on it. 'Everything will work out fine,' Phil said. 'Just . . . just not necessarily for me.'

'Then I don't think I can do it,' Tim said, feeling a sudden surge of worry and doubt. He recalled how lonely he sometimes felt back then, back before he originally created Phil. The monkey was the first thing he made when given a free go on the box. Without even realising it, Tim had just wanted a friend.

But it *was* the only option for this idea to work – he couldn't have it both ways. Tim's breathing juddered. Could he seriously do this? Would his mind actually let him? A final goodbye? He felt his lip quivering, but told himself that he wouldn't cry. He knew he mustn't – if he wasn't sure, if he wasn't *strong*, then the plan wouldn't work, his mind would betray him. He had to hide his emotions from himself – all his fears of being alone – he had to bottle them up and bury them deep, deep inside, somewhere dark and unreachable.

'I have never really fitted into this world,' Phil whispered, wiping a tiny tear from his tiny cheek. 'Maybe I belong in your imagination – maybe that is my true home? Existing has always been a conundrum for me. Far simpler, perhaps, to not.'

A few water drops landed around them, speckling the metal on the machine. A pitter-patter, cold and quick. Tim closed his eyes for a moment, but he couldn't stop the rain. Instead, he created some black umbrellas which opened above them.

Under this canopy, all three of them sat for a moment, just listening.

'I guess this is goodbye then?' Dee said. Tim was surprised to see water in her eyes too – surprised that out of the two of them, he was the one controlling his feelings.

'Farewell,' Phil said. 'I wish you both warm lives, filled with joy and wonder. May your new branches take you to beautiful places.'

Tim took a long, slow breath in and, after a few

seconds, managed to say goodbye. The ache he felt in his chest was creeping up his throat and almost snatched the word, but he pushed it back down and made a tight fist.

'Let's do it then,' Dee said with a sigh, handing Tim the reader and lifting the wire over the main part of the machine. They sat close to one another. 'Let's head on down to reset town.'

Phil sniffed, stood and jumped down on to Tim's lap, climbed up his shirt, and slid into his top pocket.

For the very last time.

Tim's eyes stung as he put the reader on his head. It was heavy and the thick cable stroked across the back of his neck and hung down his shoulder. He placed his hand on his heart, feeling Phil's beating too.

'It might not seem like it, but I do understand why you're sometimes scared,' Dee said. 'But I hope you understand why you don't need to be.'

Smiling, Tim listened to the rain for a moment – a few puddles forming on the floor at their feet. Dee put her arm round him.

There was a single button on the side of the

imagination station. Tim placed his index finger on it. 'Well,' he said. 'Here we go.'

He closed his eyes, imagined and pressed down. A digital beeping and an odd whirring sound. There was a short pause and he looked again to see a single raindrop falling past his face. It seemed suspended, held in the air, frozen in a timeless place.

'So,' Dee said, 'how will we know if it's even work—'

Chapter 1

Timothy Hart was a quiet boy. He wouldn't say he was lonely as such, but he kept himself to himself. He was most happy when he was drawing pictures in his sketchpad. And he was doing just that in the lobby at the Dawn Star Hotel – ten years old and alone, Tim was sketching a bird's-eye view of umbrellas. A muggy summer storm, warm and cold at the same time, was rumbling over Glassbridge, and yet the hotel stood proud. Even in the rain.

Elisa shrieked, telling him not to get any pencil lead on the sofa, then ran over and quickly cleaned his hands with a wet cloth. She cleaned him like he was an object, and not for the first time. She also told him to and go draw upstairs, and warned him not to touch any of the cakes in the function room.

And then, from the spray bottle she was clutching, a single drip of water landed on Tim's picture. He quickly slammed his sketchpad shut to protect his masterpiece from any further damage.

Later, up in his room, he was turning this stain into a puddle when he heard a noise, some commotion in the corridor. Through the peephole he saw it was that scientist he'd met earlier. Tim had stolen a cake from the function room, almost exclusively because Elisa had told him not to. There he'd spoken to this old professor – this grey-haired man who mumbled and said 'indeed' a lot. And, despite Tim's self-doubt, he could tell that the drawing was of umbrellas.

The man was holding a large cardboard box and fumbling to get into room nineteen, the room opposite Tim's. So Tim decided to step into the corridor and offer some help. They spoke for a while inside the professor's room. Tim asked what was in the cardboard box, but the professor refused to answer.

Tim had been so intrigued by this man that, the

moment he returned to his bedroom, he was looking again through the peephole. He was endlessly curious, you see.

The professor disappeared up the hall and Tim watched room nineteen's door gradually shut, pausing on the hinges at the last moment, dragging across the thick carpet.

But, then, clunk. It closed.

If it had got stuck, Tim thought to himself, as these doors sometimes do, would he have crept inside to see what was in that box? Impossible to say.

Never mind, Tim thought, going back to sit cross-legged on his bed with a bounce. He pulled his sketchpad on to his lap and carried on drawing. The umbrella picture was finished, so he turned to a crisp, fresh page. He clattered his pencil between his teeth for a moment, then placed it on the paper and drew the first line of his next work.

Years passed. The sketchpads piled up.

Tim grew a little taller, his artwork improved and he forgot about that professor – just another one of the thousands of guests who passed through the Dawn Star Hotel. It was a long, long time after his adoption and, slowly but surely, he and Elisa found more than just common ground. She became slightly less stressed about running the hotel, and he made a little more effort not to deliberately disobey her. Things were going well for the business too. So well that they were talking about buying another hotel – turning the Dawn Star into a brand.

Glassbridge wasn't a bad place to live, with its wonky cobbled streets, iron railings and horse statues. But the idea of moving somewhere else, even though it wasn't that far, and starting from scratch in a new home with Elisa and Chris did fill Tim with excitement.

Around the time they were first discussing this expansion, he started secondary school. Glassbridge Academy. He liked science, but art was by far his favourite subject. Not just because he was a creative sort of kid, but because he made a friend. This was a momentous event, really, and one that Elisa was keen to encourage.

It was strange, actually, how it worked out. He was

late for class on the first day, as he'd got lost, and there was a single empty seat left, next to a girl with curly blonde hair and a blue and white polka-dot pencil case. She told him her name was Dee.

During that first class, they were tasked with drawing a display of fruit on a nearby desk. Always fruit, Tim thought.

'What's that?' Dee asked, frowning at Tim's work halfway through the lesson.

'It's a finger monkey,' he said.

'I think we're supposed to draw the apples.'

'Yeah, but I want to draw this finger monkey,' Tim said.

'Fair enough.'

Sometimes, later, when they were chatting long into the night on endless summer evenings at the new hotel, Tim joked that the empty seat in art class must have been fate. They were drawn together, Tim said. But Dee always responded with something logical. She said someone else could have sat there and become her friend and she'd have never known any different. It only seemed to be a perfect turn of events looking back, she said. People spot patterns, apparently, but ignore times when it doesn't fit.

'If you have lucky pants,' she once told him, 'then you'll remember the times you wear them and something good happens. But if you wear them and no good things happen, you just ignore it and the pants stay lucky.'

'I don't have lucky pants,' Tim had said.

'Good.'

Either way, they both agreed that it was a positive thing that the empty seat was there at the back of the room that day.

Tim had just passed his thirteenth birthday when, one idle Saturday afternoon, he and Dee were having a great time doing nothing together, as only the best of friends can. They were sitting in her garden, throwing a marble back and forth to one another. The small ball of hard glass had a tiny swirl of blue through the middle.

'Biscuit,' she said, catching it. The marble came flying through the air, back to Tim.

'Um, chocolate,' Tim said, the glass ball landing in his palm.

'Milk,' Dee added.

They'd been playing word association for the past ten minutes.

'Cow.'

'Pig.'

'Horse.'

'Uh, unicorn,' Dee said, catching the marble, then flinging it back.

'Danger,' Tim said.

'No, you can't have that.' Dee was strict with the rules.

'Pointy horn.' Tim put his index finger on his forehead. 'They could be dangerous.'

'No. New round. Uh, bear.'

Tim caught the marble. 'Shark.'

'Your mind is wired up wrong,' Dee said.

'Both animals.' Tim shrugged.

'Tenuous. New round. Dog.'

'Cat?'

'Ah, yeah. That reminds me.' Dee checked her watch. 'Gotta go feed Jingles.'

'Is that some sort of code for something terrible?'

'Granddad's cat, remember? He's gone on holiday. An old-man holiday, like with walking and museums and that. Come with me, it's not far.'

'All right,' Tim said. 'Although, can I borrow your phone? Mine's flat.'

'Yeah, sure.'

Tim called Elisa and explained. 'So, yeah, I'll be back a bit later, is that cool?' he said. 'With Dee. All right, will do. Not sure, maybe like seven? Perfect, see you then. Yeah, bye, Mum.'

They left that marble, warm from their hands, resting amid the grass, then walked a short distance across town to Dee's granddad's house. She'd told Tim previously that he was a scientist, some kind of professor. However, every time she'd pried further, he apparently told her his job was actually quite boring. It was her suspicion, however, that this was untrue.

'Says he's worked on some interesting things, but not had much success,' Dee said, crouching to pour some cat food into a bowl in the kitchen. 'He's always cagey about it. But … right … in the loft …' She stood and a ginger cat arrived, rubbed against her leg, then got stuck into its dinner.

'What?' Tim said. 'What about the loft?'

It was obvious there was something she wanted to tell him, but felt she shouldn't. However, after a few seconds she took in a deep breath.

'There is a box,' she said.

Upstairs, they pulled down a ladder from a hatch and clambered into a narrow loft. It was warm up here, the summer sun coming in through a small round window and radiating off the floorboards – Tim could smell the roof's wooden struts. Cramped, but still comfortable. A nice place to be, he thought, even with the furniture and clutter.

Sure enough, there was a cube-shaped object on a table at the end of the space, right beneath the window. It was covered by a purple velvet sheet and looked special, valuable, even before they looked underneath. Carefully, Dee pulled the cover off and leant away, coughing, as the air filled with dust.

'What is it?' Tim said, wiggling his nose to avoid a sneeze.

'I dunno.' Dee shrugged. 'Some kind of machine Granddad's made.'

'What does he do again?' Tim asked, inspecting the metal and circuit boards.

'Uh, theoretical particle physics,' Dee said. 'Atom stuff? I honestly don't fully understand.'

Part of the machine caught Tim's eye.

'I think that bit goes on your head,' Dee said.

'It looks ... delicate,' Tim whispered, not wanting to touch the device. Whatever it was, it seemed like it had taken a lot of work to build.

But Dee lifted the hat-type bit and placed it on Tim's head. 'Ha, suits you,' she said.

Tim still couldn't begin to think what this thing might be. However, a green button on the top stood out. He guessed this would turn it on, if this was the kind of gadget that could be turned on, that is. Reaching out, his finger straight like the number one, the button round like a zero. Outside, the birds were singing in the trees but, beyond that, for Tim, it felt like nothing but this warm attic existed. Sometimes, when engrossed in a drawing for example, he felt as though the outside world wasn't even there. As though it was all a show put on for him, only set in motion when he was there to see it.

Now Tim's finger was hovering right over that button and he stood silently wondering whether or not he should press it.

And in that small moment, in that small attic, he imagined all the things that might happen if he did, and all the things that might happen if he didn't.